使用最 的

旅遊英語

附 **MP3**

ENGLISH FOR **TRAVEL**

出國旅遊必備寶典！從登機、出境、入境到食宿、旅遊，完全搞定！◆

張瑜凌/編著

出國旅遊必備寶典

「馬上就要出國了，現在學英文還來得及嗎？」

「我想要出國自助旅行，可是我的菜英文卻讓我很傷腦筋！」

「學了多年的英文，卻老是不敢開口説英文！」

以上是您面對要説英文時的心聲嗎？別氣餒，「使用最頻繁的旅遊英語」幫助您解決所有的英文學習問題。

為什麼您需要在出國前好好地看一看「使用最頻繁的旅遊英語」這本書呢？原因有以下幾種：

一、本書利用【基本句型】加強您面對各種情境時，能夠主動發言的英文實力。

> 🎧 基本句型
>
> ## Do you have another flight before it?
>
> 你們有在那一天之前的另一個班機嗎？

二、本書更搭配了相關情境的【實用會話】，以應付您在旅遊時所面臨的各種情境。

實用會話

A After the meal, what would you like for dessert?
正餐後，你要什麼甜點？

B May I have some cookies?
我可以吃些餅乾嗎？

A Sure. And you, sir?
當然可以。先生，你呢？

C No, thanks!
不要了，謝謝！

三、相同情境有許多不同的句子可以應付，【相關例句】便提供您相關的語句學習機會，讓您可以在同一時間，學習多元的表達方式。

相關例句

例 What's the next earliest flight for Seattle?
下一班最早到西雅圖的班機是哪一班？

四、【關鍵單字】提點您相關的重點單字，讓您學習會話的同時也能背誦單字。

五、最後，本書還提供【關鍵單字總匯】，讓您一次學習齊全相關旅遊英文的單字。

開口説英文並不難，重點是方法要正確，藉由生活情境中的需求學習英文，將會是事半功倍的學習效率。無論是登機、出境、入境，到食宿、旅遊、觀光，「使用最頻繁的旅遊英語」完全搞定！

搭飛機

在飛機上

使用最頻繁的 旅遊英語

使用最頻繁的 旅遊英語

搭車

逛街

詢問航班

使用最頻繁的 旅遊英語

Do you fly to Seattle on May 2nd?

你們有五月二日飛西雅圖的班機嗎？

🎧 實用會話

A Good morning. This is American Airlines. May I help you?
早安，這是美國航空。有什麼需要我效勞的嗎？

B Do you fly from Taipei to Seattle on May 2nd?
你們有五月二日從台北到西雅圖的班機嗎？

A Wait a moment, please. I'll see if there are any flights.
請稍等，我查一下是否有任何班機。

B Thanks.
謝謝。

A We have a nonstop flight on May 2nd.
我們有一班五月二日直達的班機。

B I see. I'd like to book this flight.
我知道了，我要訂這一個班次。

關鍵單字

fly　（飛機）飛行
flight　班機
nonstop　直達班機

Unit 2　查詢其他航班

基本句型

Do you have another flight before it?
你們有在那一天之前的另一個班機嗎？

實用會話

A Do you fly to Seattle on next Sunday?
你們有下星期天到西雅圖的班機嗎？

B Let me check. We don't have any flights on next Sunday.
讓我查一查。我們下星期天沒有任何航班。

A Do you have another flight before it?
你們有在那一天之前的另一個班機嗎？

B We have a flight on August 25th.
我們有一班八月廿五日的班機。

A I see. But I can't make it until the 30th of August.
我了解，可是我八月卅日前無法成行。

B I'm sorry, sir, that's the only flight we have.
很抱歉，先生，那一個班次是我們僅有的一個班次。

相關例句

例 What's the next earliest flight for Seattle?
下一班最早到西雅圖的班機是哪一班？

關鍵單字

check　確認
find　尋找
make it　達成、完成

使用最頻繁的 旅遊英語

 基本句型

I'd like to book flight 803 on May 2nd.

我要訂五月二日的 803 班次。

 實用會話

A
I'd like to book flight 803 on May 2nd.
我要訂五月二日的 803 班次。

B
OK. May I have your name, please?
好的！請問你的大名？

A
My name is Charlie Baker.
我的名字是查理‧貝克。

B
How do you spell your name?
你的名字怎麼拼？

A
C-H-A-R-L-I-E‧B-A-K-E-R.
C-H-A-R-L-I-E‧B-A-K-E-R.

B
OK. Please wait a moment.
好的，請稍等。

A
No problem.
沒問題。

相關例句

例
I'd like to make a flight reservation.
我要預約訂位。

例
I'd like to make a reservation for a flight to Seattle tomorrow.
我要預定明天到西雅圖的航班。

Unit 4 訂兩張機票

 基本句型

I'd like to book two seats.

我要訂兩張機票。

 實用會話

A I'd like to book two seats from Taipei to Seattle on August 25th.
我要訂八月廿五日兩個人從台北到西雅圖的機票。

B OK. There's a flight at 9 a.m. and one at 11 a.m. Which would you prefer?
好的！早上九點鐘有一班，還有一班是十一點鐘。你想要哪一個航班？

A I'd like the 9 a.m. one.
我要九點鐘的班次。

B Please give me both of your names.
請給我二位的名字。

A It's Charlie Baker and Rita Smith.
查理·貝克和瑞塔·史密斯。

B OK. Remember to be at the airport two hours before departure.
好的！記住要在離境前兩個小時到達機場。

 關鍵單字

seat　座位
prefer　偏好、較喜歡

both　兩個
departure　離境

訂直達班機

使用最頻繁的旅遊英語

 基本句型

I'd like a non-stop flight.

我要訂直達的班機。

  **實用會話**

A I want to make a reservation from Taipei to Hong Kong.
我要預約從台北到香港的機票。

B OK. When do you want to leave?
好的！你什麼時候要離開？

A I want to leave on next Wednesday.
我想要在下星期三離開。

B Let me double-check the flights. Please wait a moment.
讓我查一查航班，請稍候。

A By the way, I'd like a non-stop flight.
另外，我想要直達的班機。

B OK. A non-stop from Taipei to Hong Kong.
好的，從台北到香港的直達班機。

 相關例句

例 I'm looking for a non-stop flight from New York to Seattle.
我在找從紐約直飛西雅圖的班機。

 關鍵單字

reservation 預約
make a reservation 預約
by the way 順便、另外

Unit 6 訂轉機班機

基本句型

I'd like a stop over flight.

我要訂需要轉機的班機。

實用會話

A I'd like a stop over flight to Seattle.
我要訂到西雅圖的轉機班機。

B You can stop over in Tokyo.
你可以在東京轉機。

A Tokyo? I don't think it's a good idea.
東京？我覺得這不是個好主意。

B Or you can stop over in Hong Kong if you want.
或是你想要在香港轉機？

A I prefer to stop over in Hong Kong.
我比較喜歡在香港轉機。

B A stop over flight in Hong Kong from Taipei to Seattle. Please wait a moment.
一班從台北到西雅圖在香港轉機的班機。請稍候。

關鍵單字

stop over flight 轉機班機
stop over 中途停留(為了轉機而停留而不入境)

使用最頻繁的 旅遊英語

I'd like to book a round-trip ticket.

我要訂一張來回機票。

實用會話

A I'd like to book a round-trip ticket.
我要訂一張來回機票。

B Where do you plan to go?
你計畫去哪裡？

A From Taipei to Hong Kong.
從台北到香港。

B When do you want to depart?
你想什麼時候離境？

A During this Monday to Friday would be fine.
從這個星期一到星期五都可以。

B We have a flight on this Wednesday.
我們這個星期三有航班。

A Wednesday? OK. I'll book this flight.
星期三？好，我要訂這一個航班。

相關例句

例 Please leave the return ticket open.
回程機票請不要限定班次時間。

Unit 8 訂早晨班機

基本句型

I'd prefer a morning flight.

我偏好在早上的班機。

實用會話

A I want to fly to Chicago on the 1st of September.
我想要在九月一日飛芝加哥。

B OK. Let me see which one is available.
好的，讓我查一查哪一班航班有位子。

A I'd prefer a morning flight.
我偏好在早上的班機。

B We have Flight 861 leaves at 8:00.
我們有 861 班機早上八點鐘離境。

A Great. What time should I be at the airport?
很好。我應該什麼時候到機場？

B The check-in time is six and thirty.
報到登機的時間在六點卅分。

關鍵單字

morning flight 早晨出發的班機
leave 離開、出發
check-in time 登機報到的時間

查詢班機時刻表

使用最頻繁的 旅遊英語

 基本句型

Could you check the boarding time for me?

你能替我查班機時刻表嗎？

 實用會話

A Could you check the boarding time for me?
你能替我查班機時刻表嗎？

B Please tell me the flight number.
請告訴我班機號碼。

A It's Flight 265.
265 號班機。

B There is no Flight 265 on the boarding schedule.
265 號班機沒有在飛機的航程中。

A Really? Then I must make a mistake. Sorry.
真的？那我一定是搞錯了。抱歉。

B It's OK.
沒關係！

 相關例句

例 What time does the Flight 803 arrive?
803 號班機何時會抵達？

 關鍵單字

boarding time　班機時刻
flight number　班機號碼

Unit 10 詢問票價

What is the one-way fare?

單程票價是多少錢？

實用會話

A What is the fare from Taipei to Seattle?
從台北到西雅圖票價是多少錢？

B What class do you want?
你想要哪一種等級的座位？

A What do you have?
你們有哪些？

B We have first class and business class.
我們有頭等艙和商務艙。

A I want the first class seat.
我想要頭等艙的座位。

B The first class seat is ten thousand dollars.
頭等艙是一萬元。

A Ten thousand dollars? And what is the one-way fare?
一萬元？那麼單程票價是多少？

相關例句

例 How much is the airfare?
機票多少錢？

例 How much is the airfare from New York to Seattle?
從紐約飛西雅圖票價是多少？

變更班機

使用最頻繁的 旅遊英語

 基本句型

I'd like to change my flight.

我想要變更班機。

 實用會話

A United Airlines. May I help you?
聯合航空，你好。有什麼需要我效勞的嗎？

B This is Charlie Baker calling. I'd like to change my flight.
我是查理‧貝克，我想要變更班機。

A When do you want it to be?
你想要改到什麼時間呢？

B I'd like to reschedule the flight at 4 p.m.
我想把班機改成下午四點鐘的那班飛機。

A I'm sorry, Mr. Baker, the 4 p.m. flight is completely booked. I can put you on a waiting list.
貝克先生很抱歉，四點鐘的班機已經沒有機位了。我可以幫你排進候補名單。

B Please do it for me. And thank you very much.
請幫我(排候補名單)。還有，非常謝謝你。

 相關例句

例 I'd like to change my reservation.
我想要變更我的班機預約。

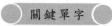 **關鍵單字**

change 改變、變更

completely 完全地

reschedule 重新變更行程

waiting list 候補名單

Unit 12 取消機位

🎧 基本句型

I'd like to cancel my reservation.

我想取消我的預約訂位。

🎧 實用會話

A Good afternoon. This is United Airlines.
午安,這是聯合航空。

B I have a reservation on the Flight 807 to Seattle tomorrow.
我訂了明天飛往西雅圖的807號班機。

A What can I do for you?
有什麼需要我效勞的嗎?

B I'd like to cancel my reservation.
我想要取消我的預約訂位。

A OK. Please tell me your name.
I'll cancel your reservation right now.
好的,請告訴我你的名字,我會立即取消你的預約。

B My name is Charlie Baker.
我的名字是查理·貝克。

🎧 相關例句

例 I need to cancel my flight.
我需要取消我的班機。

關鍵單字

cancel 取消
right now 立即、即時、馬上

Unit 13 確認機位

 **基本句型**

I'd like to reconfirm a flight.

我想再確認機位。

 實用會話

A I'd like to reconfirm a flight for Mr. Baker.
我想替貝克先生再確認機位。

B What is the flight number and date of departure, please?
請問班機號碼和起飛的日期？

A It's flight 420 to Hong Kong on October 6th at 1 p.m.
The name is Charlie Baker.
是十月六日下午一點鐘到香港的420班機，名字是查理‧
貝克。

B Please wait one moment while I confirm the flight.
請稍候，我為你做確認。

（稍後）

Thank you for waiting. Mr. Baker's seat is reconfirmed.
謝謝你的等候。貝克先生的位子已經確認無誤了。

 相關例句

例 I'd like to reconfirm my reservation.
我要再確認我的訂位機票。

例 I'd like to reconfirm my flight.
我要再確認我的班機。

關鍵單字

reconfirm　再確認
date　日期
confirm　確認、批准

登機報到

 基本句型

Where may I check in for my flight?

我可以在哪裡辦理登機手續？

實用會話

A Excuse me, could you do me a favor?
對不起，你能幫我一個忙嗎？

B Sure, what can I do for you?
好的，我能為你做什麼？

A Where may I check in for my flight?
我可以在哪裡辦理登機手續？

B Go straight ahead, and turn right then you will see the counter of United Airlines.
直走，然後右轉，你就會看到聯合航空的櫃台。

A I see. Thank you so much.
我知道了。非常感謝你。

關鍵單字

excuse me　打擾一下
favor　幫忙、協助
go straight ahead　往前方直走
turn right　右轉

Unit 15　報到劃位

搭飛機

基本句型

I'd like a window seat, please.

請給我靠窗戶的座位。

實用會話

A
I'd like to check in.
我要辦理登機。

B
OK. May I have your passport and flight ticket, please?
好的，請給我你的護照和飛機票。

A
Here you are.
給你。

B
Would you like a window or an aisle seat?
你要靠窗還是走道的座位？

A
I'd like a window seat, please.
請給我靠窗的座位。

B
Let's see. OK. There is a window seat left.
我看看。好的，剛好有剩下一個靠窗戶的座位。

相關例句

例
I'd like an aisle seat, please.
我要走道的座位。

例
I'd like an emergency exit seat, please.
請給我靠緊急出口的座位。

使用最頻繁的 旅遊英語

例 Please give me a window seat.
請給我靠窗戶的座位。

例 An aisle, please.
請給我走道的座位。

例 Can I sit at the back of the plane?
我能坐在機艙的後端嗎？

例 I'd prefer a window seat.
我偏好靠窗的座位。

關鍵單字

passport 護照

here you are 給你、這是你要的

left 剩下、遺留

window seat 靠窗的座位

Unit 16 行李超重

 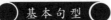 基本句型

Is my luggage overweight?

我的行李有超重嗎?

 實用會話

A Do you have any baggage?
你有行李(要托運)嗎?

B Yes, this suitcase and this carry-on bag.
有的,這個行李和這個隨身袋子。

A Put them on the scale, please.
請將它放在磅秤上。

B OK. Is my luggage overweight?
好的。我的行李有超重嗎?

A It's 95kgs. You have to pay 200 dollars for excess baggage.
95公斤。你要付台幣200元的超載費。

 相關例句

例 It's at least 20 pounds overweight.
它至少超重20磅。

手提行李

 基 本 句 型

I'll keep this bag as my hand baggage.

這是我的隨身行李。

 實 用 會 話

A Do you have any baggage to check in?
你有任何行李要托運的嗎？

B No. I'll keep this bag as my hand baggage.
沒有，這個是我的隨身行李。

A Your carry-on bag is too big and overweight.
你隨身的袋子太大又超重。

B I know, but they are so fragile.
我知道，但是他們都是易碎的。

A Sorry, sir, I'm afraid you'll have to check in your bag.
先生，很抱歉，你的袋子恐怕要辦理托運。

關 鍵 單 字

hand-carry　手提的
overweight　　　超重的

基本句型

I have two pieces of baggage to check in.

我有兩件行李要托運。

 實用會話

A How many pieces of baggage do you have?
你有多少件行李？

B I have two pieces of baggage to check in.
我有兩件行李要托運。

A Please put them on the scale.
請將它們放在磅秤上。

（秤過行李後）
Here is your boarding pass. The baggage tag is attached to the flight ticket.
這是你的登機證，行李標籤附在機票上。

B Thank you.
謝謝你。

相關例句

例 I have these suitcases to check in.
這些是我要托運的行李。

關鍵單字

tag　標籤
be attached to　附在～之上、和～貼在一起
boarding pass　登機證

使用最頻繁的 旅遊英語

基 本 句 型

What is the boarding time?

登機時間是什麼時候？

實 用 會 話

A Here is your boarding pass and passport.
這是你的登機證和護照。

B Thank you.
謝謝你。

A Don't be late to get on the plane.
別太晚去搭飛機。

B What is the boarding time?
登機時間是什麼時候？

A At six o'clock, thirty minutes before departure.
六點鐘，是離境前的三十分鐘。

B Thanks a lot.
多謝了！

相 關 例 句

例 What time can we start boarding?
我們什麼時候可以開始登機？

詢問登機地點

搭飛機

基本句型

Where is the boarding gate?

要在哪裡登機？

實用會話

A Where is the boarding gate?
要在哪裡登機？

B What is your boarding gate number?
你的登機門是幾號？

A It's Gate 7.
是七號登機門。

B Gate 7... Let's see. It's over there.
七號登機門...我看看！在那個地方。

A I see. Thank you very much.
我知道了，非常感謝你。

相關例句

例 Where is the boarding gate for American Airlines?
美國航空的登機門在哪裡？

例 Excuse me, where should I board?
請問，我應該到哪裡登機？

例 Is Gate 7 this way?
七號登機門是往這個方向嗎？

確認登機門號碼

使用最頻繁的 旅遊英語

 基本句型

What's the gate number?

登機門是幾號？

 實用會話

A What's the gate number?
登機門是幾號？

B You can find the boarding gate number on the boarding pass.
你可以在登機證上找到登機門的號碼。

A Really? Let me see.
真的？我看看。

B It's on the right side. Do you see it?
在右邊。看見了嗎？

A Oh, I found it. The Gate Number is 7. Thank you very much.
喔，我找到了。登機門號碼是七號。非常感謝你。

B You are welcome.
不客氣。

 相關例句

例 Where is the Gate 7?
七號登機門在哪裡？

例 I'm at the wrong gate.
我走錯登機門了。

Unit 22　表明自己要轉機

基本句型

I'm in transit to New York.

我要轉機到紐約。

實用會話

A Excuse me. I'm in transit to New York.
請問一下，我要轉機到紐約。

B What can I do for you?
需要我幫什麼忙的嗎？

A How can I get to the connecting flight counter of American Airlines?
我要如何到美國航空的轉機櫃臺？

B It's over there, next to the bank.
就在那裡，銀行的旁邊。

A Thank you so much.
非常謝謝你！

相關例句

例 I'm a transit passenger.
我是轉機乘客。

例 I'm a transit passenger for Flight AE709.
我是搭乘AE709航班的轉機乘客。

例 I'm a transit passenger for this flight.
我是搭乘這個航班的轉機乘客。

轉機的相關問題

使用最頻繁的 旅遊英語

🎧 基本句型

How do I transfer to New York?

我要如何轉機到紐約？

🎧 實用會話

A What can I do for you?
有什麼需要我協助的嗎？

B How do I transfer to New York?
我要如何轉機到紐約？

A OK. Let me see your transit card.
好的！給我看看你的轉機證。

B Sure. Here you are.
好！在這裡。

A Seven thirty p.m. Your boarding gate is 6.
晚上七點半，你的登機門是六號。

🎧 相關例句

例 How long is the stopover?
停留的時間會是多長？

例 Are there any duty-free shops in the waiting room?
候機室裡有沒有免稅商店？

例 When are we going to leave here?
我們什麼時候要離開這裡？

例 How do I get to terminal four?
四號航廈要怎麼走？

確認轉機的航班

 基本句型

I'm connecting with AE709.

我要轉搭 AE709 班機。

 實用會話

A Good morning, madam.
早安，女士。

B Good morning. I'm connecting with AE709.
早安。我要轉搭 AE709 班機。

A OK. May I have your passport and visa, please?
好的。請給我你的護照和簽證。

B Here you are.
在這裡。

A Here is your boarding card and the boarding time is at four o'clock.
這是你的登機證，登機時間是四點鐘。

 相關例句

例 If the flight is late, we'll miss our connection.
如果班機延遲，我們會錯過我們的轉機。

例 I'm continuing on to New York.
我要繼續飛往到紐約。

尋找座位

使用最頻繁的 旅遊 英語

 基本句型

My seat number is 36A.

我的座位號碼是 36A。

 實用會話

A Welcome aboard, sir. May I help you find your seat?
先生，歡迎搭乘。我來幫忙找你的座位好嗎？

B Please. My seat number is 36A.
麻煩你了！我的座位號碼是 36A。

A About halfway down this aisle, row 22.
往走道走下去，第二十二排。

B Is it an aisle seat?
這是靠走道的座位嗎？

A No, it's not. It's a window seat.
不，不是的。是靠窗戶的座位。

B Thanks a lot.
多謝！

 相關例句

例 Excuse me, but where is my seat?
請問一下，我的座位在哪裡？

例 Which way should I go?
我要往哪個方向走？

Unit 26 請求協尋座位

基本句型

Can you tell me where my seat is?

你能告訴我我的座位在哪裏嗎？

實用會話

A Excuse me, can you tell me where my seat is?
對不起，能告訴我我的座位在哪裡嗎？

B Sure. What is your seat number?
當然，你的座位是幾號？

A It's 36A.
是 36A。

B OK. Down this aisle, to you right. It's a window seat.
好的！往走道走下去，在你的右邊。是個靠窗的位子。

相關例句

例 Could you show me where my seat is?
可以告訴我我的座位在哪裡嗎？

例 I couldn't find my seat.
我找不到我的座位。

關鍵單字

down　　往南方地

請求帶位服務

使用最頻繁的 旅遊英語

基本句型

Would you please take me to my seat?

能請你幫我帶位嗎？

實用會話

A Excuse me, would you please take me to my seat?
抱歉，能請你幫我帶位嗎？

B Of course. May I see your boarding pass?
當然好的。請給我看你的登機證。

A Here you are.
在這裡。

B Let's see... 36A, this way, please. It's an aisle seat.
It's next to this gentleman's.
我看看，36A，這邊請。這是個靠走道的座位。
在這位先生旁邊。

A I see. Thank you very much.
我知道了！非常謝謝你。

相關例句

例 Will you show me to my seat, please?
請帶我到我的座位好嗎？

關鍵單字

take me to 帶我至某處　　　way 路途、方向

of course 當然　　　aisle seat 靠走道的座位

質疑對方坐錯座位

在飛機上

 基本句型

This is my seat.

這是我的座位。

 實用會話

A Excuse me. Is this 36A?
抱歉，這是 36A 嗎？

B 36A? No, it's 35A.
36A？不是的，這是 35A。

A I'm afraid you have my seat.
你恐怕是坐了我的座位。

B Really? Let me see. Oops, it's 36A. I'm so sorry.
真的？我看看，哎呀，這是 36A！真是抱歉！

A It's all right.
沒關係！

 相關例句

例 Excuse me. I believe you are sitting in my seat.
抱歉打擾了，你坐了我的座位。

例 Someone is sitting in my seat.
有人坐了我的位子。

關鍵單字

afraid　恐怕、擔心
all right　沒關係

要求更換座位

 基本句型

Can I change my seat?

我能不能換座位？

 實用會話

A What can I do for you?
有什麼需要我幫忙的嗎？

B Yes. Can I change my seat? My wife and I are separated.
有的！我能不能換座位？我太太跟我的位子被分開了。

A Sure, let's see what I can do.
好的，我看看我能作什麼。

B And can we move to the smoking area?
我們能移到吸煙區嗎？

A Sure. I'll arrange it for you right now.
當然可以。我馬上替二位安排。

 相關例句

例 I want to change my seat.
我想要換座位。

例 Can I change my seats with you?
我可以和你換座位嗎？

例 Is this seat vacant?
這個座位是空的嗎？

例 Would you mind changing seats with me?
你介意和我換座位嗎？

要求更換座位

在飛機上

例　Can I move to the non-smoking area?
我可以移到非吸煙區嗎？

關鍵單字

wife　妻子
smoking area　吸煙區
separated　被迫分開、分離
arrange　安排、安置

要求提供幫助

🎧 基本句型

Do you have a Chinese newspaper?

你們有中文報紙嗎？

 實用會話

A May I help you?
需要我幫忙嗎？

B Yes! Do you have a Chinese newspaper?
有的！你們有中文報紙嗎？

A Yes, we do.
是的，我們有。

B And may I have a pack of playing cards?
那我可以要一副撲克牌嗎？

A No problem, sir. What else do you need, sir?
先生，沒問題的！好的，先生，你還需要其他東西嗎？

B I want a blanket, please.
我想要一條毛毯。

 相關例句

例 Do you have an earphone?
請問有沒有耳機？

例 Does any attendant speak Mandarin?
請問有沒有會說國語的空服員？

例 How can I use this?
這個要怎麼使用？

要求提供幫助

例 Do you know the local time in Seattle?
你知道西雅圖當地的時間嗎？

例 May I have something to read?
有什麼可以閱讀的嗎？

關鍵單字

newspaper 報紙
playing card 撲克牌

在飛機上

Unit 31 提供毯子

 基本句型

May I have a blanket?

我能要一條毯子嗎？

 實用會話

A Excuse me, I feel cold. May I have a blanket?
對不起，我覺得有一些冷，我能要一條毯子嗎？

B Sure. Would you also like a pillow?
好的，請稍等。你是否也需要枕頭？

A Sure, by the way, could you get me some beer, too?
好啊，你能順便也給我一些啤酒嗎？

B Certainly. I'll be right back with you.
當然好！我馬上回來。

A Thank you so much.
真的是非常感謝你。

 相關例句

例 May I have a blanket and a pillow?
可以給我一張毯子和枕頭嗎？

例 I need this.
我需要這個。

Unit 32 詢問盥洗室的方位

 基本句型

Which way is the lavatory?

盥洗室在哪個方向？

 實用會話

A Excuse me, which way is the lavatory?
對不起，盥洗室在哪個方向？

B It's down the aisle, to the left.
就在走道最後面，在左邊！

A I see. Thank you very much.
我了解了，謝謝你。

B You are welcome.
不客氣。

A Is this vacant?
(廁所)是空的嗎？

C No, it's occupied.
不是，(裡面)有人。

相關例句

例 Where is the bathroom?
洗手間在哪裡？

例 Is the lavatory now occupied or vacant?
廁所現在是有人在使用還是空的？

例 Excuse me. I have to go wash my hands.
請問一下，我要去洗手間。

使用最頻繁的 旅遊英語

 基本句型

Could you tell me how to fill it out?
你能告訴我怎麼填寫嗎？

 實用會話

A Do you need the Customs Form?
你需要海關申報表嗎？

B Yes, please.
我需要，麻煩你了。

A Here you are.
給你。

B Could you tell me how to fill it out?
你能告訴我怎麼填寫嗎？

A Sure. Write down your name in this blank.
當然好。在這一空白欄填上你的名字。

 相關例句

例 Could you tell me how to fill out this immigration form?
你可以告訴我怎麼填寫入境卡嗎？

例 What is this?
這是什麼？

Unit 34 放置行李

基本句型

Where should I put this baggage?

我應該把行李放哪裡？

實用會話

A Excuse me, where should I put this baggage?
請問一下，我應該把行李放哪裡？

B You can store extra baggage in the overhead cabinet.
你可以把多出來的行李放在上方的行李櫃裡。

A Over here?
在這裡嗎？

B Yes. Let me help you with it.
是的。我來幫你處理。

A I can arrange it by myself. Thank you.
我可以自己來。謝謝你！

相關例句

例 Could you help me get my bags down?
可以幫忙拿我的袋子下來嗎？

例 Would you please put this bag in the overhead bin for me?
可以請你幫我把袋子放在頭頂的置物箱中嗎？

例 Please help me put my baggage up.
請幫忙把我的袋子放上去。

打開話匣子

 基本句型

You look familiar.

你看起來很面熟耶！

 **實用會話**

A Excuse me. That's my seat.
抱歉，那是我的位子。

B Okay.
好的。

A You look familiar. Are you Rita?
妳看起來很面熟，妳是瑞塔嗎？

B Yes, I am. And you are...?
是的，我就是。而你是…？

A I'm Charlie. Remember me? We worked together five years ago.
我是查理。記得我嗎？我們五年前共事過。

B Charlie? What a coincidence.
查理？真是巧合。

 相關例句

例 Hi, how are you?
嗨，你好嗎？

例 Good morning.
早安！

自我介紹

 基本句型

Hi, I'm Charlie.

嗨，我是查理。

 實用會話

A Hi, I'm Charlie.
嗨，我是查理。

B My name is Rita. Nice to meet you, Charlie.
我是瑞塔，很高興認識你，查理。

A Nice to meet you too.
我也很高興認識你。

B This is an interesting novel, isn't it?
這是一本有趣的小說，不是嗎？

A Yes, it is. I really can't put it down.
是啊，的確是。我真的是愛不釋手。

 相關例句

例 My name is Charlie.
我的名字是查理。

例 Please call me Charlie.
請叫我查理就可以了！

例 This is my husband Charlie.
這是我的先生查理。

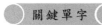 關鍵單字

meet 認識、見面　　　　　interesting 有趣的、好玩的
novel 小說

基本句型

It's nice talking to you.

很高興和你聊天。

 實用會話

A It's nice talking to you.
很高興和你聊天。

B Nice talking to you too.
我也很高興和你聊天。

A By the way, do you mind if I ask your phone number?
對了，你介不介意我問你的電話號碼？

B Not at all. My phone number is 86473663.
一點也不會(介意)。我的電話號碼是 86473663。

A And here is mine.
這是我的電話號碼。

B Let's keep in touch.
讓我們保持聯絡吧！

 相關例句

例 It's good to talk to you.
很高興和你聊天。

關鍵單字

ask 詢問
mine 我的（東西、物品等）
touch 觸摸、接觸、交往
keep 保持

Unit 38 飛機上的餐點

基本句型

What do you have?

你們有提供哪些餐點？

實用會話

A What would you like for dinner?
晚餐你想吃什麼？

B What do you have?
你們有提供哪些餐點？

A We have chicken and beef.
我們提供雞肉和牛肉。

B I'd like beef, please.
我要吃牛肉，謝謝。

A OK. Here you are.
好的，這是你的餐點。

B And may I have a glass of water?
我能要一杯水嗎？

相關例句

例 What kind of meals do you have?
你們有提供什麼餐點？

例 Do you have beef?
你們有提供牛排嗎？

例 Is that free?
免費的嗎？

使用最頻繁的 旅遊英語

例　Do you have instant noodles?
你們有提供泡麵嗎？

例　I'd like beef, please.
我要牛肉，謝謝！

例　This one, please.
我要這個，謝謝！

關鍵單字

dinner　晚餐、正餐
chicken　雞肉
beef　牛肉

Unit 39 是否有素食餐點

 基本句型

Do you have a vegetarian meal?

你們有提供素食餐點嗎？

 實用會話

A　What would you like for dinner, sir? Beef or chicken?
　　你晚餐要吃什麼？牛肉或雞肉？

B　Do you have a vegetarian meal?
　　你們有提供素食餐點嗎？

A　We have rice and noodles. Which one do you prefer?
　　我們有飯和麵，你喜歡哪一種？

B　I would like to have noodles, please.
　　請給我麵。

相關例句

例　Is this a vegetarian meal?
　　這是素食餐點嗎？

在飛機上

飛機上的飲料

使用最頻繁的 旅遊英語

 基本句型

Do you have any cold drinks?

你們有提供冷飲嗎？

實用會話

A Excuse me. I'm a little thirsty. Do you have any cold drinks?
對不起，我有一點口渴，你們有提供冷飲嗎？

B What would you want to drink?
你想要喝什麼？

A May I have a glass of orange juice?
我能要一杯柳橙汁嗎？

B OK. I'll right back with you.
好的，我馬上回來。

And you, sir? Coffee or tea?
先生你呢？咖啡或茶。

C Coffee, please.
請給我咖啡。

 相關例句

例 May I have something to drink?
我可以喝一些飲料嗎？

例 Can I have another drink?
我可以再喝一杯嗎？

指定飲料

Do you have lemonade?

你們有檸檬汁嗎？

A What would you like to drink?
你想要喝什麼？

B Do you have lemonade?
你們有檸檬汁嗎？

A I'm afraid not. But we have apple juice.
How would you like it?
很抱歉我們沒有，但是我們有蘋果汁，你想要喝嗎？

B Well, it sounds good.
這個嘛...聽起來不錯。

A Good. I'll be right back soon.
很好，我馬上回來。

相關例句

例 May I have some water?
我可以喝水嗎？

例 May I have some more tea, please?
請再給我一些茶。

例 May I have more coffee?
請再給我一些咖啡。

使用最頻繁的 旅遊英語

例 I'd like some wine.
我想要喝一些酒。

例 Do you have orange juice?
你們有柳橙汁嗎？

關鍵單字

lemonade 檸檬汁
apple juice 蘋果汁
sound 聽見（聲音）、(某事)聽起來

Unit 42　想要嘔吐

在飛機上

基本句型

I feel like vomiting.

我快要吐了。

實用會話

A Madam, are you all right? You look pale.
女士，妳還好吧？妳看起來臉色好蒼白。

B I don't feel good. I feel like vomiting.
我覺得不舒服，我快要吐了。

（A對空服員C說話）

A This lady doesn't feel well.
Do you have airsickness bags?
這位女士覺得不舒服。你們有嘔吐袋嗎？

C Here you are.
(嘔吐袋)在這裡。

相關例句

例 I still feel like throwing up.
我還是很想吐！

關鍵單字

pale 臉色蒼白
airsickness bag 嘔吐袋
feel like 覺得快要…

Unit 43 覺得不舒服

 基本句型

I feel airsick.

我覺得暈機。

 實用會話

A Are you all right? You look terrible.
你還好吧？你看起來很糟糕。

B I feel airsick.
我覺得暈機了。

（A對空服員C說話）

A Excuse me, may I have some medicine for airsickness?
抱歉，我能要一些治療暈機的藥嗎？

C Sure. Here you are.
當然可以！給你。

B May I have a glass of hot water? Not too hot, please.
我可以要一杯熱開水嗎？不要太熱。

 相關例句

例 I'm feeling awful.
我覺得很不舒服。

例 I have a headache.
我頭痛！

例 I feel sick.
我覺得不舒服！

Unit 43　覺得不舒服

例　I don't feel well.
我覺得不舒服！

例　I feel much better.
我覺得好多了！

關鍵單字

terrible　糟糕的、臉色不好的
airsick　暈機的
airsickness　暈機症狀
not　too　不太～

請求提供醫藥服務

使用最頻繁的 旅遊英語

 基本句型

I'd like some medicine.

我需要一些藥。

 實用會話

A Sir, are you OK?
先生，你還好吧？

B I don't know. I have a headache.
我不知道。我頭痛。

A Do you need some medicine?
你需要一些藥嗎？

B Yes, I'd like some medicine, please. Thank you.
好的，我需要一些藥。謝謝你。

A Here is the medicine and a glass of water.
來，這是藥和一杯水。

B Thanks. It makes me feel better.
謝謝。它讓我覺得好多了。

 相關例句

例 Please give me some airsickness pills.
請給我一些暈機藥。

Unit 45 在海關遞交證件

基本句型

This is my passport and visa.

這是我的護照和簽證。

實用會話

A Passport and visa, please.
(請給我)護照和簽證。

B This is my passport and visa.
這是我的護照和簽證。

A May I see your round-trip ticket?
我可以看你的回程機票嗎？

B Sure. Here you are.
當然可以。在這裡。

A Please take off your sun glasses and hat.
請將太陽眼鏡和帽子脫下。

B Sure.
好的！

A What's the purpose of your visit?
你此行的目的是什麼？

關鍵單字

take off 脫下（衣服、帽子、眼鏡等）
sun glasses 太陽眼鏡
hat 帽子

解釋出國的目的

基本句型

I'm here for sightseeing.

我來這裡觀光。

實用會話

A What's the purpose of your visit?
你此行的目的為何？

B I'm here for sightseeing.
我來這裡觀光。

A Where are you going to stay during this time?
這段時間你要在哪裡投宿？

B I'm going to stay at the Grand Hyatt Hotel.
我會住在凱悅飯店。

A OK. Here is your passport. Have a nice trip.
好的，這是你的護照。（祝你）旅途愉快！

相關例句

例 To see friends.
探望朋友！

例 Just touring.
單純旅遊！

例 It's for business.
我是來出差的。

例 For study.
來唸書的。

例　I'm just passing through.
我只是過境！

例　I'm leaving for New York tonight.
我今晚要過境到紐約。

例　I'm on my way to New York.
我要過境去紐約。

回答停留時間

使用最頻繁的 旅遊英語

 基本句型

I'll stay here for one more week.

我會在這裡停留一個多星期。

 實用會話

A How long will you be staying in Seattle?
你會在西雅圖停留多久？

B I'll stay here for one more week.
我會在這裡停留一個多星期。

A Do you have any relatives or friends here?
在這裡有親戚或朋友嗎？

B No, I don't.
沒有。

A OK. Here is your passport. Have a nice trip.
好的，這是你的護照，(祝你)旅途愉快。

 相關例句

例 Five days.
五天！

例 I'm planning to stay here for 10 days.
我打算要在這裡待十天。

在海關

🎧 **基本句型**

Do you have anything to declare?

有沒有要申報的物品？

🎧 **實用會話**

A
Passport and visa, please.
請給我你的護照和簽證。

B
Here you are.
在這裡。

A
Do you have anything to declare?
有沒有要申報的物品？

B
Yes, I have two bottles of wine to declare.
是的，我有兩瓶酒要申報。

A
Please fill up this declaration.
請填申報單。

(B 填完後)

It's four hundred for them.
這些總共是四百元。

🎧 **相關例句**

例
Yes, I do. Here is my form.
有的，我有（要申報）。這是我的申請單。

例
I have a carton of cigarettes.
我有一條香菸。

使用最頻繁的 旅遊英語

例 I have nothing to declare.
我沒有要申報的東西。

關鍵單字

declare　向(海關、稅務局)申報(納稅品、所得稅等)
bottle　瓶、一瓶(的量)
declaration　(納稅品的)申報(表)

基本句型

Should I open my baggage?

需要我打開行李嗎？

實用會話

A Good day, sir.
先生，你好。

B Should I open my baggage?
我應該打開行李嗎？

A Yes, please.
是的，麻煩你。

B OK. Here you are.
好的。請看。

A What are these?
這些是什麼？

B They are presents for my parents.
這是給我父母的禮物。

相關例句

例　Where is the customs inspection?
海關檢查站在哪裡？

關鍵單字

good day　祝你今天愉快、你好（一種打招呼的方式）

解釋行李內的物品

 基本句型

Personal stuff.

私人物品。

 實用會話

A Open your baggage, please.
請打開你的行李。

B OK. Here you are.
好的，請看。

A What are those boxes?
那些盒子是什麼？

B My medicines. Those medicines are prepared for this tour.
我的藥。那些藥物是為了這趟旅行而準備的。

A How about that?
那些呢？

B Personal stuff.
私人物品。

 相關例句

例 Those are presents for my family.
是給我家人的禮物。

例 They are gifts for my friends.
他們是要給我朋友的禮物！

例 It's fruit.
是水果！

Unit 50 解釋行李內的物品

例 I have some duty-free items.
我有一些免稅商品。

關鍵單字

personal 個人的、私人的
prepare 準備
tour 旅行、行程
stuff (泛指)東西、物品、事物

使用最頻繁的 旅遊英語

 基本句型

Where is the baggage claim area?

哪裡是行李提領區？

實用會話

A Excuse me, would you tell me where I could have my baggage?
抱歉，你能告訴我可以在哪裡提領我的行李嗎？

B You could find your baggage at the baggage claim.
你可以在行李提領區找到你的行李。

A Where is the baggage claim area?
哪裡是行李提領區？

B Do you see the sign over there?
Follow it and you will see it in front of you.
有看到那邊的標誌嗎？跟著標誌走你就會看到在你面前。

A I see. Thank you.
我瞭解了，謝謝你。

相關例句

例 Excuse me, where is the baggage claim area?
請問一下，哪裡是行李提領區？

例 Can I get my baggage right now?
我可以現在提領行李嗎？

例 This is my baggage claim tag.
這是我的行李牌。

行李提領

例　That's it. I saw my baggage.
　　這個就是！我看見我的行李了！

關鍵單字

baggage claim　行李提領區
follow　循著…方向、跟隨

使用最頻繁的旅遊英語

基本句型

Where is the Lost Baggage Service?

行李遺失申報處在哪裡？

實用會話

A I can't find my baggage. What can I do?
   我找不到我的行李。我應該怎麼辦？

B You have to go to the Lost Baggage Service.
   你要去行李遺失處理中心。

A Where is the Lost Baggage Service?
   你知道行李遺失申報處在哪裡嗎？

B Maybe you could go to the Custom Information Center.
   也許你可以去旅客諮詢中心（詢問）。

A I'll try. Thanks anyway.
   我會試一試。總之，還是謝謝你。

相關例句

例 Please help me find my baggage.
    請幫我尋找我的行李。

例 I can't find my baggage.
    我找不到我的行李。

例 My suitcase hasn't come out yet.
    我的行李還沒有出來。

例　This is my baggage claim tag, but I can't find my baggage.

這是我的行李牌，但是我找不到我的行李。

例　How soon will you find my baggage?

你們有多快可以找到我的行李？

關鍵單字

Lost Baggage Service　行李遺失處理中心

Custom Information Center　旅客諮詢中心

使用最頻繁的 旅遊英語

 基本句型

I can't find my baggage.

我找不到我的行李。

 實用會話

A I can't find my baggage. What should I do first?
我找不到我的行李。我應該先作什麼？

B May I see your baggage tag?
我可以看一下你的行李牌嗎？

A Here you are.
在這裡。

B OK. Please fill out this claim form.
好的，請先填這張申訴表格。

A What is this for?
這是作什麼用的？

B We'll inform you as soon as we find your baggage.
只要我們找到你的行李時，我們會通知你。

 相關例句

例 My bags were delayed.
我的行李被耽擱了。

例 One of my bags hasn't come.
我有一件袋子還沒有出來。

例 My baggage seems to be missing.
我的行李好像遺失了！

行李

例　What do I do if I can't find my baggage on arrival?
如果我抵達的時候找不到行李怎麼辦？

例　I didn't find my baggage.
我找不到我的行李。

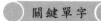
關鍵單字

claim form　申訴表
as soon as　當～時候、一旦～時

行李遺失的數量

使用最頻繁的 旅遊英語

 基本句型

We may have lost some baggage.

我們可能遺失一些行李了！

 實用會話

A Excuse me, could you do me a favor?
抱歉，你能幫我一個忙嗎？

B Yes. What can I do for you?
好的，我能為你作什麼？

A We may have lost some baggage.
我們可能遺失一些行李了！

B How many bags are missing?
少了幾件袋子？

A There are two. They are red and with wheels.
(總共)有兩件，它們都是紅色有輪子的。

B OK. I'll see what I can do for you.
好的！我看看能幫上什麼忙。

相關例句

例 I'm missing three suitcases.
我少了三件行李。

關鍵單字

missing 遺失、不見、消失
with wheels 有輪子的、附輪子的

詢問兌換貨幣處

兌換外幣

 基本句型

Can you tell me where to change money?

你能告訴我在哪裡兌換外幣嗎？

實用會話

A Oh, shit! I forgot to change money.
喔！糟糕。我忘了兌換錢幣了。

B It's terrible. You'd better change it quickly.
真糟糕，你最好快一點去換。

A Can you tell me where to change money?
你能告訴我在哪裡兌換外幣嗎？

B You can go to the Currency Exchange.
你可以去兌換錢幣處。

A Where is it?
在哪裡？

B It's right behind you.
就在你後面。

相關例句

例 Where is the Currency Exchange?
錢幣兌換處在哪裡？

例 Where can I exchange money?
我可以到哪裡兌換錢幣？

例 Where can I find a bank around here?
這附近哪裡有銀行？

使用最頻繁的 旅遊英語

例 Do you know where I can get this changed?
你知道我可以在哪裡換開嗎？

例 I want to break this 1,000 bill.
我要換開這一張一千元。

關鍵單字

change 兌換（貨幣）
Currency Exchange 錢幣兌換處
break 兌換（貨幣）

兌換匯率

 基本句型

What is the exchange rate now?

現在匯率是多少？

實用會話

A How may I help you?
有什麼需要我協助的嗎？

B I want to exchange money into Taiwan dollars.
我想要兌換台幣。

A What currency you want to convert from?
你想要用哪一種貨幣兌換？

B From U.S. dollar. What is the exchange rate now?
從美金(換成台幣)。現在匯率是多少？

A The exchange rate from U.S. dollar to Taiwan dollar is thirty-four point five.
現在美金兌換成台幣的匯率是卅四點五。

B I see. Thanks for your help.
我瞭解了！謝謝你的幫助。

 相關例句

例 What is the exchange rate today?
今天的匯率是多少？

兌換貨幣

使用最頻繁的 旅遊英語

 基本句型

I'd like to change these dollars into U.S. dollars.

我要把這些兌換成美金。

 實用會話

A May I help you?
需要我效勞嗎？

B I'd like to change these into U.S. dollars.
我想要把這些兌換成美金。

A OK. Please fill up this form first.
好的，請先填寫這份申請單。

B Here is the form and money.
這是申請單和錢。

A You want to change NT$5,000 into U.S. dollars?
你想要將台幣五千元換成美金？

B Yes.
是的。

A Here is US$147.
這裡是一百四十七元美金。

 相關例句

例 Could you break this $100?
你可以找開這張一百元嗎？

兌換貨幣

例 Can you break this into small money?
你可以兌換成小鈔嗎？

例 Can you break this 1,000 bill?
你可以將這張一千元換成零錢嗎？

關鍵單字

fill up 填寫
form 表格
small money 小鈔、零錢

紙鈔兌換成零錢

使用最頻繁的 旅遊英語

 基本句型

Would you please break this $200?

請將二百元換成零錢。

實用會話

A Excuse me, I'd like to exchange money.
抱歉，我要兌換錢幣。

B OK. What would you like to exchange?
好的！你要兌換什麼？

A Would you please break this $200?
請將二百元美金換成零錢。

B How much do you want to exchange?
你想兌換多少？

A I want to break this 200 dollars into 4 twenties, 3 tens and the rest in coins.
我想要將兩百元兌換成四張二十元、三張十元，剩下的是零錢。

相關例句

例 Could you include some small change?
可以包括一些零錢嗎？

例 Can you cash this traveler's check?
你們可以兌換旅行支票嗎？

例 Could you break this $ 1.00?
你可以換開這一美元嗎？

辦理入住手續

🎧 (基本句型)

I'd like to check in.

我要登記住宿。

🎧 (實用會話)

A Welcome to Grand Hyatt Hotel. What can I do for you?
歡迎光臨凱悅飯店。有什麼需要我為你效勞的嗎？

B I'd like to check in.
我要辦理住宿登記。

A Do you have a reservation?
你有預約（訂房）嗎？

B Yes. My name is Chandler Smith.
有的。我的名字是錢德・史密斯。

A Mr. Smith, Let me check it for you.
史密斯先生，讓我為你查一下。

（稍後）

OK. Mr. Smith, here is your room key
好的，史密斯先生，這是你的房間鑰匙。

🎧 (相關例句)

例 Check in, please.
我要辦理入住手續。

例 Check in, please. My name is Jack Smith.
我要辦理入住手續。我的名字是傑克・史密斯。

辦理入住手續

例 What time can I check in?
我什麼時候可以辦理入住手續？

例 Is it too early to check in now?
現在辦理入住手續會太早嗎？

例 Is my room ready? Can I check in early?
我的房間準備好了嗎？我可以早一點入住嗎？

Unit 60 預約訂房

 基本句型

I have a reservation for 2 nights.

我已訂了兩晚的住宿。

實用會話

A I'd like to check in.
我要辦理入住手續。

B I'm sorry, sir, I couldn't find your name.
先生，很抱歉，我找不到你的名字。

A But I have a reservation for 2 nights and here is the confirmation slip.
但是我有預約兩晚的住宿，還有這是我的確認單。

B All right. I'll make sure again.
好的！我再確認一次。

（稍後）

Sorry, sir, I found your name.
Here is your key to Room 156.
先生，很抱歉，我找到你的名字了。
這是156號房的鑰匙。

相關例句

例 I had a reservation at the airport today.
我今天在機場有預約訂房。

例 I'd like to book a single room tonight.
我要預約今晚的一間單人房。

預約訂房

使用最頻繁的 旅遊英語

例 I made a reservation in Taiwan last Friday.
我上週五在台灣有預約訂房。

關鍵單字

confirmation slip 確認單
make sure 確認無誤

住宿時間

🎧 基本句型

I plan to stay here for two nights.

我計畫要待在這裡兩晚。

🎧 實用會話

A Madam, may I help you?
夫人，需要我的協助嗎？

B Yes. I'd like to check in.
是的，我要登記住宿。

A Did you make a reservation?
你有預約住宿嗎？

B No, I don't.
沒有，我沒有。

A Sure, madam. How many nights will you be staying?
好的，女士，你想要住幾晚？

B I plan to stay here for two nights.
我計畫要待在這裡兩晚。

A May I have your name, please?
請給我你的名字。

🎧 相關例句

例 I'm going to stay for four nights.
我要住四晚。

增加住宿天數

 **基本句型**

I want to stay for two more nights.

我想再多住兩晚。

 **實用會話**

A Excuse me.
打擾一下！

B Yes, may I help you?
是的，有什麼需要我協助的嗎？

A I missed my plane this morning, so I want to stay for two more nights.
我錯過今早的飛機了，所以我想要再多住兩晚。

B May I have your name, sir?
先生，請問你的名字？

A I'm Jack Smith of room six eighteen.
我是618號房的傑克·史密斯

B Mr. Smith, I already change your record.
You could stay here until this Friday.
史密斯先生，我已經更改你的記錄了，你可以住到這個星期五為止。

關鍵單字

miss 錯過、錯失、遺失
already 已經、早就、早已
record 記錄、登錄

Unit 63 退房

 基本句型

When is the check-out time?

什麼時候可以退房？

 實用會話

A Excuse me, when is the check-out time?
抱歉，什麼時候可以退房？

B It's before eleven thirty.
十一點三十分之前。

A I see. What if I can't make it before that?
I'm afraid I'd be late.
我瞭解。萬一我到時趕不到怎麼辦？我擔心我會遲到。

B Don't worry about it. Just let us know when you are going to check out.
不用擔心。只要讓我們知道你什麼時候要退房。

A I really appreciate it.
我真的很感謝。

B You are welcome.
不客氣。

相關例句

例 Check out, please.
麻煩你，我要退房。

例 Can I check out now?
我可以現在退房嗎？

使用最頻繁的 旅遊英語

例 When can I check out?
我什麼時候可以退房？

關鍵單字

late 遲到的、晚到的
appreciate 感謝、感激

訂單人床的房間

基本句型

I'd like a room for one.

我要一間單人房。

實用會話

A May I help you?
需要我的協助嗎？

B Yes, I'd like a room for one.
是的，我要一個單人房。

A May I have your name, please?
請給我你的名字。

B My name is Charlie Baker.
我的名字是查理・貝克

A OK. Mr. Baker, here is your key to Room 245.
好的，貝克先生，這是你245號房的鑰匙。

B Thank you.
謝謝你。

相關例句

例 Do you have a room for one?
你們有單人房嗎？

例 I'd like a single room.
我要單人房。

訂雙人房

使用最頻繁的 旅遊英語

 基本句型

We'd like a room for two.

我們要雙人房。

 實用會話

A Welcome to Sheraton Hotel. How may I be of service?
歡迎光臨喜來登飯店。我能為你服務嗎？

B We'd like to check in.
我們要登記住宿。

A Would you like a double room or two single rooms?
你要雙人房還是二間單人房？

B We'd like a room for two.
我們要雙人的房間。

A OK. How about single separate beds?
好的，兩張分開的單人床房間可以嗎？

B That would be fine.
很好。

 相關例句

例 I'd like a room for two with separate beds.
我要一間有兩張床的雙人房間。

例 A double room, please.
請給我雙人房。

Unit 66 早上叫醒服務

I'd like to have a wake-up call at 8 am.

我要設定早上八點鐘電話叫醒。

實用會話

A Can I have a morning call tomorrow?
我能設定明天早上叫醒的服務嗎？

B Of course you can. What time do you want?
當然可以。你想要什麼時間（叫醒）？

A I'd like to have a wake-up call at 8 a.m.
我要設定早上八點鐘電話叫醒。

B 8 o'clock in the morning.
We'll call you at 8 o'clock tomorrow.
早上八點鐘。我們會在明天八點鐘打電話給你。

A By the way, I'd like a wake-up call every morning.
對了，我每一天都要早上叫醒(的服務)。

B No problem, sir.
沒問題的，先生。

關鍵單字

morning call　早晨叫醒
wake-up call　叫起床的電話

要求多加一張床

使用最頻繁的 旅遊英語

 基本句型

I'd like an extra cot for Room 243.

我要在 243 房多加一張床。

 實用會話

A Custom Service Center. How may I be of help?
客戶服務中心，你好。需要我的協助嗎？

B Yes, I'd like to an extra cot for Room 243.
是的，我要在 243 房多加一張床。

A Yes, sir. We'll arrange it for you right away.
好的，先生。我們會盡快為你安排。

B How much does it charge?
這要收多少錢？

A It's NT$800 for each extra cot. We'll charge you when you check out.
每加一張床要台幣八百元。我們會在你退房時收費。

B Good. Thank you.
很好！謝謝你。

 相關例句

例 Could you put in a cot?
可以加一張床嗎？

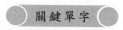 關鍵單字

Custom Service Center　客戶服務中心

送餐食到房間

基本句型

I'd like to order room service, please.

我要送食物到房間的服務。

實用會話

A Custom Service Center, may I help you?
客戶服務中心，你好，需要我的協助嗎？

B I'd like to order room service, please.
我要食物送到房間的服務。

A What do you want to order?
你想要點什麼？

B Would you bring us a bottle of champagne?
你能帶一瓶香檳給我們嗎？

A OK. A bottle of champagne. What else do you want, sir?
好的！一瓶香檳。先生，你還需要其他的東西嗎？

B Let's see, and I want a chicken sandwich.
我想想，還有我要一份雞肉三明治。

相關例句

例 Will you send up two cups of coffee, please?
請你送兩杯咖啡上來，謝謝！

例 Please bring me a pot of tea.
請帶給我一壺茶。

使用最頻繁的 旅遊英語

例 Who is it?
哪一位？（有人敲門時）

關鍵單字

order 訂購、選購
bottle 瓶、罐
champagne 香檳
else 其他的

供應餐點

基本句型

What time is breakfast served?

早餐什麼時候供應？

實用會話

A Here is your key and breakfast coupon.
這是你的鑰匙和早餐券。

B What time is breakfast served?
早餐什麼時候供應？

A It's between 7 a.m. and 10 a.m.
在早上七點鐘和十點鐘之間。

B Where should I go for the breakfast?
我應該去哪裡用餐？

A It's at the Summer Restaurant on 2nd floor.
在二樓的夏季餐廳。

相關例句

例 Where is the dining room?
餐廳在哪裡？

例 What time do you start serving breakfast?
你們什麼時候供應早餐？

例 Are you still serving meals?
你們還有供應餐點嗎？

例 I lost my breakfast coupons.
我把早餐券弄丟了。

使用最頻繁的 旅遊英語

 基本句型

Do I have any messages?

我有任何的留言嗎？

 實用會話

A Good morning, Mr. Baker.
早安，貝克先生。

B Good morning. Do I have any messages?
早安。我有任何留言嗎？

A Yes, there is a package from a young lady.
有的，一位年輕的女士送來一個包裹。

B It's my younger sister. Did she say anything?
那是我的小妹。她有說什麼嗎？

A She asked you to give her a call when you are not busy.
她請你有空的時候打電話給她。

B Is that all? I thought she was supposed to give me a letter.
就這樣？我以為她應該會給我一封信。

 相關例句

例 Could you call a cab for me? I'm going to the airport.
可以幫我叫計程車嗎？我要去機場。

例 Where can I access the internet?
我可以在哪裡上網？

要求櫃台協助

例 I have to check my e-mail.
我要收電子郵件。

例 I need to make an overseas call.
我要打國際電話。

例 How can I place a collect call?
我要怎麼打對方付費電話？

例 Where can I send this fax?
哪裡可以傳真？

例 Can I store my luggage here?
我可以把我的行李放在這裡嗎？

例 I'd like to pick up bags.
我要取回我的袋子。

關鍵單字

message　訊息、留言
package　包裹

衣服送洗的服務

 基本句型

Do you have laundry service?

你們有衣物送洗的服務嗎？

實用會話

A Room service.
(這裡是)客房服務中心。

B Do you have laundry service?
你們有衣物送洗的服務嗎？

A Yes, we have, sir.
先生，我們有(這項服務)。

B Wonderful. This is room 916.
太好了。這是916號房。

A OK. We'll get it in a few minutes.
好的，我們會在幾分鐘之內去拿。

B I'm going to catch my train. Could you make it quickly?
我要趕火車。你能快一點嗎？

A No problem, sir. We'll do it right now.
先生，沒問題的。我們馬上(派人)去做。

 相關例句

例 I have some laundry.
我有衣物要送洗。

例 I'd like to send my suit to the cleaners.
我有一件西裝要送洗。

衣服送洗的服務

例 I'd like these clothes laundered.
我要送洗這些衣物。

例 Could you come and pick it up?
你們可以來收（待洗衣物）嗎？

例 When will it be ready?
什麼時候可以洗好？

例 Can I have my shirt cleaned by tonight?
今晚之前可以洗好我的襯衫嗎？

關鍵單字

laundry 　洗衣、待洗的衣物
clothes 　衣服、衣物
catch 　追趕(火車、汽車等)

遇到問題

 基本句型

Our hair dryer is broken.

我們的吹風機壞了。

 實用會話

A Guest services.
(這裡是)客房服務中心。

B Our hair dryer is broken.
我們的吹風機壞了。

A What's the matter with it?
發生什麼問題？

B I don't know. It's not working anymore.
我不知道！就不能運作啦！

A OK. We'll send someone to fix it.
好的。我們會派人過去。

B Can you please hurry?
你能快一點嗎？

A He'll be there in five minutes.
五分鐘內就會有人過去。

 相關例句

例 There is no hot water.
沒有熱水！

例 I'd like to change my room.
我想要換房間。

例　The lock of my room is broken.
我房間的鎖壞了！

例　There is something wrong with the toilet.
馬桶有一些問題！

例　I locked myself out.
我把自己反鎖在外了！

例　I left my key in the room.
我把鑰匙遺忘在房間裡了。

例　I can't find any towels in my room.
我房間裡沒有毛巾！

例　There seems to be a problem with the shower.
淋浴間好像有一點問題。

例　Can you send someone up to have a look?
可以請你派個人上來瞧一瞧嗎？

例　This is for you.
這是給你的（小費）。

Unit 73 住宿費用

 基本句型

How much per night?

(住宿)一晚要多少錢？

 實用會話

A We would like a double room.
我們要一間雙人房。

B OK. How would you like the room facing the swimming pool?
好的。你覺得房間面對游泳池如何？

A Wonderful. And how much per night?
很好。(住宿)一晚要多少錢？

B It's 3,500 dollars per night.
(住宿)一晚要三千五百元。

A Do you have any cheaper rooms?
你們有便宜一點的房間嗎？

B Certainly.
當然有。

相關例句

例 How much is the room?
房價是多少？

例 How much will it be?
會是多少錢？

例 Do you have any rooms less expensive?
有沒有沒那麼貴的房間？

例 How much are doubles?
雙人房的房價是多少？

關鍵單字

facing 面對
swimming pool 游泳池
per night 每一晚

其他額外的費用

使用最頻繁的 旅遊英語

 基本句型

Please charge it to my room.

請將帳算在我的房間費用上。

 實用會話

A May I help you?
需要我效勞嗎？

B Yes, I'd like a bottle of champagne.
是的，我要一瓶香檳。

A OK. Anything else, sir?
好的。先生，還需要其他東西嗎？

B Let me see...no, that's all.
我想想...，沒有，就這樣。

A How do you like to pay it, sir?
先生，你要怎麼付錢呢？

B Please charge it to my room. It's room 714.
請將帳算在我的房間費用上，房間號碼是七一四。

 相關例句

例 Does the room rate include breakfast?
住宿費有包括早餐嗎？

例 Are the service charges and tax included?
是否有包括服務費和稅金？

例 Are there any additional charges?
是否有其他附加費用？

Unit 74　其他額外的費用

例　I'm afraid there is something wrong with the bill.
這個帳單恐怕有點問題耶！

例　What are these other charges?
這些是什麼費用？

例　I didn't make those calls.
我沒有打這些電話。

例　I had nothing to do with it.
這和我沒有關係。

肚子餓

 基本句型

I'm so starving!

我好餓！

 實用會話

A I'm so starving!
我好餓！

B It's dinnertime.
晚餐時間到了。

A Can we take a break and find a good restaurant?
我們能不能休息一下然後找一間好的餐廳？

B But I'm not hungry.
可是我不餓啊！

A You're not? You didn't eat anything since this morning.
你不會（餓）？你從今天早上起就沒吃任何東西了。

B I'm on a diet.
我在減肥。

 相關例句

例 I'm not so hungry.
我不是很餓！

例 Are you hungry?
你餓了嗎？

例 What would you like to eat?
你想吃什麼？

肚子餓

例 Let's grab something to eat.
我們隨便找點東西吃吧！

關鍵單字

starving 飢餓
take a break 短暫休息、休憩片刻
on a diet 在減肥中、在節食中

餐點的種類

 基本句型

I want to eat hamburger.

我想吃漢堡。

 **實用會話**

A What would you like to eat?
你想吃什麼？

B I want to eat hamburger.
我想吃漢堡。

A How about McDonald's?
麥當勞怎麼樣？

B I hate MacDonald's. Hey, there is a Kentucky Fried Chicken across the street.
我討厭麥當勞。嘿，對面街道有一家肯德基炸雞。

A Let's go over there.
走吧！我們去那裡。

 相關例句

例 Let's eat sandwiches for dinner.
我們晚餐就吃三明治吧！

例 I want to have fried chicken.
我想要吃炸雞。

例 How about Japanese food?
要不要吃日本料理？

解決三餐

例 I'll have toast and bacon, and omelets for breakfast!
我要培根土司還有蛋餅當早餐。

例 What's the difference between this and that?
這個和那個有什麼不同？

詢問想吃什麼

使用最頻繁的 旅遊 英語

 基本句型

What would you like for dinner?

你晚餐想吃什麼？

實用會話

A Look! That cake looks so delicious.
看！那塊蛋糕看起來好好吃。

B I know what you meant. You could eat a horse, right?
我知道你的意思。你餓到可以吃下一匹馬，對吧？

A Yes. Can we have dinner now?
是啊！我們現在可以吃晚餐了嗎？

B What would you like for dinner?
你晚餐想吃什麼？

A I miss Chinese home cooking.
我想念中式家常菜。

B Chinese food? Are you sure? I thought you were tired of it.
中國料理。你確定？我以為你厭煩了。

 相關例句

例 What do you want to have for breakfast?
你早餐想吃什麼？

關鍵單字

be tired of... (對某事)感到厭煩、厭倦

邀請朋友一起用餐

 基本句型

Would you like to have dinner with us?

你想和我們一起吃晚餐嗎？

實用會話

A We really have to leave now.
我們真的該走了。

B Come on. Would you like to have dinner with us?
不要這樣嘛！你想和我們一起吃晚餐嗎？

A We would love to. But we have other plans.
我們很想。但是我們有其他計畫。

B You do? What a pity.
你們有（計畫）了？真可惜。

A Maybe next time.
也許下一次。

B How about Friday? It's before you are back to Taiwan.
星期五如何？就在你們回台灣之前。

相關例句

例 Would you like to have lunch with us?
要不要和我們一起吃午餐？

關鍵單字

next time 下一次
how about～ 對(某事或某物)你覺得如何(一種徵詢的語句)

使用最頻繁的 旅遊英語

基本句型

I want a table for 2, please.

我要兩個人的位子。

實用會話

A Welcome to Four Seasons Restaurant.
歡迎光臨「四季餐廳」。

B I want a table for 2, please.
我要兩個人的位子。

A Smoking or non-smoking area?
吸煙區或非吸煙區？

B Non-smoking, please.
麻煩你，非吸煙區。

A You have to wait for about 20 minutes for the non-smoking area.
要非吸煙區的話，你們大概要等廿分鐘。

B That's all right. We can wait.
沒關係，我們可以等。

相關例句

例 We reserved a table for five for seven o'clock.
我們預訂了七點鐘五個人的位子。

例 My name is Charlie. I have a reservation.
我的名字是查理。我有訂位。

預約餐廳的訂位

例 We had a reservation. My name is Charlie.
我們已經有預約了。我的名字是查理。

例 I'd like to make a reservation for tonight.
我想預訂今晚的位子。

關鍵單字

smoking area 吸煙區
non-smoking area 非吸煙區

Unit 80 確認用餐的人數

 基本句型

I am alone.

我一個人。

 實用會話

A Do you have a reservation?
你有訂位嗎？

B Yes, I made a reservation at six.
有的，我訂了六點鐘的位子。

A For how many, please?
你要訂幾人(的位子)？

B I am alone.
我一個人。

A This way, please.
這裡請。

B Thank you.
謝謝。

 相關例句

例 I want a table for five, please.
我要五個人的位子。

例 Five people, please.
五個人，謝謝！

詢問餐廳是否客滿

解決三餐

 基本句型

Do you have a table available?

現在還有空位嗎？

實用會話

A May I help you?
需要我效勞嗎？

B Do you have a table available?
現在還有空位嗎？

A For how many people, please?
請問有幾個人？

B There are four of us.
我們有四個人。

A I'm afraid you have to wait for 20 minutes.
你恐怕要等廿分鐘。

B Thank you. We'll try another restaurant.
謝謝你！我們會試另一家餐廳。

相關例句

例 Can we have a table?
有空位嗎？

例 We don't have a reservation.
我們沒有訂位！

對座位不滿意

 基本句型

We'd like the seats near the window.

我們想要靠窗的位子。

 實用會話

A Your table is ready, sir. This way, please.
先生，你的位子準備好了！請這邊走。

B OK.
好的。

A Please be seated.
請坐。

B Sorry, but we'd like the seats near the window.
抱歉，我們想要靠窗的位子。

A I'm sorry, sir. We don't have other seats available.
很抱歉，先生。我們沒有其他空位了。

B OK. Forget it.
好吧，算了。

相關例句

例 Could we take this seat?
我們可以坐這個位子嗎？

例 Could we have a quiet table?
我們能不能選安靜的座位？

例 It's too noisy here.
這裡太吵了。

對座位不滿意

例 Could you arrange another table for us?
可以幫我們安排另外的座位嗎？

關鍵單字

be seated　坐下
near　靠近、鄰近
forget　忘記、不把～放心上、忽略

Unit 83 確認何時點餐

使用最頻繁的 旅遊英語

基本句型

Sorry, we are not ready yet.

對不起，我們還沒有準備好（要點餐）。

實用會話

A Are you ready to order?
你們準備好點餐了嗎？

B Sorry, we are not ready yet.
對不起，我們還沒有準備好（要點餐）。

A Take your time. I'll be right back with you.
慢慢來。我待會再來。

B Thank you.
謝謝你。

相關例句

例 Sorry, we have not decided yet.
對不起，我們還沒有決定好。

例 Sorry, we're not ready to order.
抱歉，我們還沒有準備要點餐。

例 Yes, please.
是的，（要點餐了）麻煩你囉！

關鍵單字

take your time 慢慢來不要著急的意思

Unit 84　要求看菜單

 基本句型

May I see the menu?

我可以看菜單嗎？

 實用會話

A Please be seated, ladies and gentlemen.
請坐，各位先生、小姐。

B Thank you. May I see the menu, please?
謝謝你。我可以看菜單嗎？

A Sure. Here you are.
好的，請看。

B We'll let you know if we are ready to order.
等我們準備好點餐的時候會讓你知道。

A No problem. Take your time.
沒問題。你慢慢來吧！

B Thank you.
謝謝你。

 相關例句

例 Let me see the menu.
給我看菜單。

例 May I see the menu again?
我可以再看一次菜單嗎？

使用最頻繁的 旅遊英語

 基本句型

I'd like to order Sirloin Steak.

我要點沙朗牛排。

 實用會話

A Are you ready to order?
你準備好要點餐了嗎？

B Yes, we are ready.
是的，我們準備好了。

A What do you want for the entree?
你的正餐要點什麼？

B I'd like to order Sirloin Steak.
我要點沙朗牛排。

A How about you, madam?
女士，妳呢？

C I will try the Roast Chicken.
我要試試烤雞。

 相關例句

例 I'll have a T-bone steak for my main dish.
我主餐要點丁骨牛排。

例 What kind of soup do you have?
你們有什麼湯？

例 How does it taste?
味道如何？

有關於餐點

例 Is it a big portion?
份量很多嗎?

entree 餐點、正餐

使用最頻繁的 旅遊英語

🎧 基本句型

What is today's special?

今天的特餐是什麼？

🎧 實用會話

A What is today's special?
今天的特餐是什麼？

B It's Fillet Steak.
是菲力牛排。

A It sounds good. I'll try it.
聽起來不錯，我點這一個。

C I'd like New York Steak.
我要點紐約牛排。

B I'm sorry, but we don't have New York Steak now.
很抱歉，我們現在沒有紐約牛排。

C OK. Then I want the Picatte.
好吧！那我要點煎豬排。

 相關例句

例 I think I will try today's special.
我要試試今天的特餐。

例 What is today's special to the house?
今天餐廳的特餐是什麼？

例 What's the chef's suggestion?
主廚推薦的料理是什麼？

解決三餐

例　What's the served with the steak?
牛排的副餐是什麼？

例　Sorry, can I change my order?
抱歉，我可以更改我的餐點嗎？

 關鍵單字

special　(菜單上的)特色餐點

牛排的烹調熟度

使用最頻繁的 旅遊英語

基本句型

Well done, please.

請給我全熟。

實用會話

A Both of us would like Fillet Steak.
我們兩個都要菲力牛排。

B How do you like your steak cooked?
你的牛排要幾分熟？

A Well done, please.
請給我全熟。

B How about you, sir?
先生，你呢？

C Medium, please.
請給我五分熟。

相關例句

例 Rare, please.
三分熟，謝謝！

例 Well done, please.
全熟，謝謝！

關鍵單字

cooked 烹調

Unit 88 侍者的推薦

 基本句型

What would you recommend?

你有什麼好的推薦嗎？

 實用會話

A What is today's special to the house?
今天餐廳的特餐是什麼？

B It's Italian food.
是義大利食物。

A What would you recommend?
你有什麼好的推薦嗎？

B The Italian Seafood is the best one.
義大利海鮮食物是最棒的。

A OK. I'll try this one.
好，我要試這一種。

B How about the soup? Seafood soup or beef soup?
湯呢？海鮮湯或牛肉湯？

A Beef soup, please.
我選牛肉湯，謝謝！

相關例句

例 What is your suggestion?
你的建議是什麼？

點和他人相同餐點

 基本句型

Make it two.

（這個餐點）點兩份。

實用會話

A Are you ready to order?
你準備好要點餐了嗎？

B I'd like Sirloin Steak. It's my favorite.
我要沙朗牛排。這是我的最愛。

C Make it two.
點兩份。

A OK. Two Sirloin Steak. How about the dessert?
好的，兩份沙朗牛排。點心呢？

B I want pudding.
我要布丁。

C I'll try ice cream.
我要點冰淇淋。

 相關例句

例 Same here.
我也是點一樣的。

例 Can I have the same dish as that?
我可以點和那個一樣的餐點嗎？

 關鍵單字

make it two 點兩份(點和前一個點菜者相同餐點)

一般飲料

 基本句型

I want something cold for drink.

我想要喝點冷飲。

實用會話

A Would you like something to drink?
你要不要來點飲料？

B I want something cold for drink.
我想要喝點冷飲。

A How about a cup of rose tea? It's very popular.
喝杯玫瑰茶怎麼樣？這個很受歡迎。

B It sounds terrific. I'll take it.
聽起來很棒。我就點這個。

C I'd like coffee, please.
我要點咖啡，謝謝。

B OK. I'll be right back.
好的，我馬上回來。

相關例句

例 I'd like the brandy.
我要白蘭地酒。

例 Beer, please.
請給我啤酒。

使用最頻繁的 旅遊英語

 基本句型

May I have some cookies?

我可以吃些餅乾嗎？

 實用會話

A After the meal, what would you like for dessert?
正餐後，你要什麼甜點？

B May I have some cookies?
我可以吃些餅乾嗎？

A Sure. And you, sir?
當然可以。先生，你呢？

C No, thanks!
不要了，謝謝！

 相關例句

例 I will skip the dressing, please.
我不用醬汁，謝謝！

關鍵單字

cookie 餅乾
and you 你呢？（表示詢問意見的意思）

Unit 92　確認點完餐

 基本句型

That's all for us.

我們就點這些了。

 實用會話

A　Both of us would like Sirloin Steak.
我們兩個都要沙朗牛排。

B　Two Sirloin Steak. Is that all?
兩份沙朗牛排。就這樣嗎？

A　That's all for us.
我們就點這些了。

C　Oh, by the way, may I have some more puff?
喔，順便一提，我可以再多要一些泡芙嗎？

B　Sure. Anything else?
好的。還有沒有要其他餐點？

C　No, that's all. Thanks.
沒有，就這樣了！謝謝！

 相關例句

例　Thanks. That's all.
謝謝！這樣就好！

使用最頻繁的 旅遊英語

 基本句型

Could you serve us as soon as possible?

你能不能盡快為我們上菜？

 實用會話

A Is that all for order?
你點的就這些嗎？

B Yes. That's it.
是的，就這些。

A OK. The meal will be served soon.
好的，餐點會盡快為你送上。

B Could you serve us as soon as possible?
你能不能盡快為我們上菜？

A No problem.
沒問題。

相關例句

例 Could you rush our order, please?
可以快一點送餐嗎？

關鍵單字

as soon as possible 盡快～、盡量～

請同桌者遞調味料

 基本句型

Please pass me the salt.

請遞鹽給我。

 實用會話

A So we have to be airport by 4 o'clock next morning?
所以我們明天早上四點鐘前就要到達機場？

B Exactly. Don't be late.
沒錯，不要遲到。

（C打斷A與B的談話）

C Excuse me, please pass me the salt.
對不起，請遞鹽給我。

B Sure, here you are.
當然好，給你。

C Thank you. Go ahead.
謝謝你。(你們)繼續(說話)。

關鍵單字

next morning 明天早上
late 遲到
pass 傳遞、遞某物給某人

使用最頻繁的 旅遊 英語

 基本句型

I drop my fork.

我的叉子掉到地上了！

 實用會話

A Waiter!
(男)服務生！

B May I help you?
需要我為你效勞嗎？

A I drop my fork. May I have a new one?
我的叉子掉到地上了！我能要一支新的嗎？

B I'll change a new one for you.
我會幫你換支新的。

A Thanks.
謝謝。

C And would you bring us some bread?
還有，你能再給我們一些麵包嗎？

 相關例句

例 This meat is overcooked.
這個肉煮得太老了！

例 I didn't order this dish.
我沒有點這道菜！

例 Could we have an extra bowl?
我們可以多要一個碗嗎？

整理桌面

解決三餐

 基本句型

Would you clear the table?

你可以整理一下桌子嗎？

 實用會話

A Waitress!
女服務生！

B Yes?
是的？

A Would you clear the table for us?
你可以為我們整理一下桌子嗎？

B Sure.
好的。

（B 正在收拾桌上的餐盤）

A Oh, leave that left. I'm still working on it.
喔，那個留下來。我還在用。

B Sorry.
抱歉！

 相關例句

例 Please take it away.
請收走！

關鍵單字

clear 清潔、整理
work on 繼續用餐中、某活動持續進行中

使用最頻繁的旅遊英語

🎧 **基本句型**

We have finished it.

我們用完了。

🎧 **實用會話**

A Excuse me. May I have some water?
抱歉,我能要一些水嗎?

B Sure. And have you finished or still working on it?
當然好。你用完餐了嗎? 還是要繼續用?

A We have finished it.
我們用完了。

B Can I take your plate?
我可以收盤子了嗎?

A Please. Thank you.
麻煩你,謝謝。

B You are welcome.
不客氣。

🎧 **相關例句**

例 Leave that left.
那個留下來。

例 I'm still working on it.
我還在用餐。

解決三餐

基本句型

Bill, please.

服務生，買單。

實用會話

A I'm full.
我飽了。

B Shall we go now?
我們能走了嗎？

A OK, let's go.
好了，我們走吧！

B Bill, please.
請買單。

C Cash or credit cards?
用現金還是信用卡(付帳)？

B Credit cards.
信用卡(付帳)。

相關例句

例 Check, please.
請結帳。

例 Can I have the check, please?
請結帳！

例 Do you accept credit cards?
你們有收信用卡嗎？

例　Do you take American Express?
你們有收美國運通卡嗎？

例　I'll pay cash.
我付現金！

例　Where to pay?
要去哪裡結帳？

分開結帳

 基本句型

Let's go Dutch.

讓我們各付各的吧！

 實用會話

A Would you like to separate your checks?
要分開的帳單嗎？

（B 對 C 說）

B I'll treat you.
我請你。

C No, I insist on paying the bill.
不，我堅持付帳。

B Come on. Let's go Dutch.
好了，讓我們各付各的吧！

C Good idea.
好主意。

A Would you pay it by cash or credit cards?
你要用現金還是信用卡付帳？

B Credit card, please.
信用卡，麻煩了。

 相關例句

例 Let's split the bill.
我們分攤費用吧！

分開結帳

例 We'd like to pay separately.
我們要分開結帳!

關鍵單字

treat　請客、對待
insist on　堅持某事

Unit 100 請客

 基本句型

I'll take care of the bill.

我來付帳！

 實用會話

A Check, please.
請結帳。

B Do you want separate checks?
你們要不要分開付帳？

A I'll take care of the bill.
我來付帳！

C Thank you. You are so kind to me.
謝謝！你真好！

A May I have the receipt please?
可以給我收據嗎？

B Sure, wait a moment, please.
當然可以，請稍等！

 相關例句

例 Dinner is on me.
晚餐算我的！

例 I'll pay the bill.
我來付錢！

例 This is on me.
算我的。

請客

使用最頻繁的 旅遊英語

例 I'll treat you.
我請你。

關鍵單字

take care 負責
receipt 收據

帳單明細

 基本句型

Is the service charge included?

有包含服務費嗎？

 實用會話

A It's seven hundred and seventy dollars.
總共七百七十元。

B Is the service charge included?
有包含服務費嗎？

A Yes. It's included 10 % service charge.
是的，包含百分之十的服務費。

B I see. I'll pay it by cash. Here you are.
我要用現金付錢。錢給你。

A OK. Wait a moment.
好的，請稍等。

B Keep the change.
不用找零錢了。

 相關例句

例 Does it include the service charge?
有包含服務費嗎？

例 Does it include a tip?
有包含小費嗎？

例 This is for you.
（小費）給你！

關鍵單字

service charge 服務費
pay it by cash 用現金付錢
keep 保留、留下

Unit 102　決定要內用或外帶

 基本句型

To go, please.

（我要）外帶，麻煩你。

解決三餐

 實用會話

A I'd like a cup of coffee, please.
我要一杯咖啡，謝謝。

B Stay or to go?
要這裏用還是外帶？

A To go, please.
（我要）外帶，麻煩你。

B It's 60 dollars, please.
六十元。

A Here is 100 dollars.
這是一百元。

B Here is your coffee and changes.
這是你的咖啡和零錢。

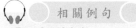 相關例句

例 A chicken sandwich to go, please.
我要外帶一份雞肉三明治。

例 A cup of coffee. For here, please.
我要一杯咖啡，內用，謝謝！

例 I'll eat here.
我要在這裡吃！

143

使用最頻繁的旅遊英語

例　For here, please.
這裡用餐，謝謝！

關鍵單字

a cup of　一杯～（喝茶或咖啡用的）

Unit 103 速食餐點醬料

基本句型

Ketchup, please.

（請給我）蕃茄醬。

實用會話

A I'd like McChicken Nuggets.
我要點麥克雞塊。

B What sauces would you like?
你要什麼醬料？

A Ketchup, please.
(請給我)蕃茄醬。

B Here is your order.
這是你的餐點。

A Can I have an extra ketchup?
我能多要一份蕃茄醬嗎？

B Sure. Here you are.
當然可以，這是你要的。

相關例句

例 I'll have extra ketchup.
我要多要一份蕃茄醬。

例 Ketchup and mustard, please.
請給我蕃茄醬和芥末醬。

點速食店的飲料

使用最頻繁的 旅遊英語

 基本句型

I want Coke.

我要可樂。

 實用會話

A	Do you want any drinks? 你要點飲料嗎？
B	I want Coke. 我要可樂。
A	Larger or regular? (要)大杯或普通杯？
B	Regular, please. (請給我)普通杯。
A	How about you, sir? 先生，你呢？
C	No, thanks. 不要，謝謝。

 相關例句

例	Coke, please. （我要）可樂，謝謝！
例	A Coke, please. 一杯可樂，謝謝！
例	Two coffees, please. 兩杯咖啡，謝謝！

點速食店的飲料

例 I'd like a cup of black, please.
請給我一杯紅茶。

關鍵單字

larger　大的
regular　普通的

咖啡的奶精和糖包

基本句型

Would you like cream or sugar?

你要奶精還是糖？

實用會話

A I'd like a cup of coffee, please.
請給我一杯咖啡。

B Would you like cream or sugar?
你要奶精還是糖？

A I'd like both, thank you.
我兩種都要，謝謝。

B How about you, sir?
先生，你呢？

C Coffee, two sugars and two cream, please.
請給我咖啡、兩包糖和兩包奶精，謝謝。

B I see.
我知道了。

關鍵單字

cream　奶精
sugar　糖、細糖

 基本句型

Do you have any tour brochure?

你們有市內旅遊手冊嗎？

實用會話

A Good afternoon, sir. How may I help you?
午安，先生，需要我的協助嗎？

B Could you tell me where the custom tour center is?
你能告訴我哪裡有旅客旅遊中心嗎？

A It's right on the corner of the first street.
就在第一條街的角落。

B Thank you.
謝謝你。

(稍後在旅客旅遊中心)

Do you have any tour brochure?
你們有市內旅遊手冊嗎？

C It's over there. Help yourself.
就在那裡，請自取。

 相關例句

例 Can I have a tour brochure?
我可以要一份旅遊手冊嗎？

例 I'm lost. Where am I now?
我迷路了！我現在人在哪裡？

使用最頻繁的 旅遊英語

例 Where can I get a map of the city?
我可以在哪裡索取本市的地圖？

例 Could you please look for it for me?
可以請你幫我找嗎？

例 I've lost my passport.
我遺失護照了！

例 I need your help.
我需要你的幫忙。

例 Please help me with it.
請幫我這個忙。

關鍵單字

custom tour center　旅客旅遊中心
on the corner　在角落
tour brochure　旅遊導覽手冊
help yourself　請對方自己動手拿的意思

參加旅遊團

 基本句型

I'd like to join the full-day city tour.

我想要參加市內一日遊的行程。

 實用會話

A How may I help you?
需要我的協助嗎？

B I'd like to join the full-day city tour.
我要參加市內的一日遊行程。

A OK. Here is the registration form. Please fill it up.
好的，這是登記表格，請先填寫。

B What kind of tour do you have?
你們有哪一種行程？

A There are 3 tours, Disneyland, Museum, and Casino.
有三種旅遊團，迪士尼樂園、博物館和賭場。

B I'd like to join the Casino.
我要參加賭場的行程。

 相關例句

例 We'll take that course.
我們就參加那個行程。

例 I want to join that two-day course.
我想要參加那個兩天行程。

例 I'd love to try it.
我想試試看。

使用最頻繁的 旅遊英語

例　I'd rather go on a half-day tour.
　　我寧願要參加半天的旅遊行程。

例　How long are we staying here?
　　我們會在這裡待多久？

例　What time should we return to the bus?
　　我們什麼時候要回去公車上？

例　Would you take a picture of us?
　　可以請你幫我們拍照嗎？

關鍵單字

join　參加、加入
full-day　全日的、一日的
city tour　市內旅遊團

Unit 108 旅遊團種類

Which tour do you suggest?

你建議哪一種旅遊團？

 實用會話

A How may I help you?
需要我的協助嗎？

B I'd like to join the city tour.
我想要參加市內旅行團。

A How long will you stay in New York?
你會在紐約停留多久？

B Before this Friday. Which tour do you suggest?
星期五之前。你建議哪一種旅遊團？

A How about two-day tour? It includes Disneyland and sea cruise.
兩日遊行程如何？包括迪士尼樂園和海上旅遊。

B It sounds interesting. I'll think about it. Thank you.
聽起來不錯，我考慮一下。謝謝你。

 相關例句

例 What kind of tour do you have?
你們有哪一種行程？

例 Do you have any package tours?
你們有任何套裝旅遊行程嗎？

使用最頻繁的 旅遊英語

例 Do you have any sightseeing tours of the city?
你們有本市的觀光行程嗎？

例 Do you have any exciting tours?
你們有刺激一點的行程嗎？

例 Does this tour include the art gallery?
行程中有包含(參觀)畫廊嗎？

 關鍵單字

suggest 提出建議
interesting 有趣的

觀光

🎧 基本句型

Do you have any idea about good sightseeing places?

你知道有什麼好的觀光景點嗎？

🎧 實用會話

A I plan to stay here for 4 days. What kind of city tour should I take?
我計劃在這停留四天。我應該參加哪一種行程？

B How do you like sightseeing buses?
你覺得市區觀光巴士如何？

A I'd love to try. Do you have any idea about good sightseeing places?
我想試試看。你知道有什麼好的觀光景點嗎？

B You can visit every art gallery or museum. It's only 400 dollars.
你可以參觀每一個美術館和博物館，只要四百元。

🎧 相關例句

例 Could you make an itinerary for me?
可以幫我安排行程嗎？

例 I want to visit these scenic spots.
我要參觀這些景點。

例 What time does the tour start?
旅遊團幾點開始？

推薦觀光景點

例 Which tour do you recommend?
你建議什麼旅遊團？

例 Are there any good places for a day trip by train?
有沒有什麼地方是可以搭火車一天觀光的？

例 Are there any amusement parks around here?
這附近有沒有遊樂園？

例 Is there a guided tour in Chinese at the museum?
博物館有沒有中文導覽？

關鍵單字

sightseeing bus 觀光巴士
art gallery 美術館

基本句型

Is the tour all-inclusive?

旅遊行程包括所有的費用嗎？

 實用會話

A I'd like to join the sea cruise tomorrow.
我要參加明天的遊艇行程。

B OK. It's 2,000 dollars for one person.
好的，每一個人兩千元。

A Is the tour all-inclusive?
旅遊行程包括所有的費用嗎？

B Yes, round-trip fare and meals are included.
是的，包括來回車資和餐費。

A Is there a pick-up service at the hotel?
有沒有到飯店的接送呢？

B Yes, the guide will pick you up.
是的，導遊會接送你。

 相關例句

例 How much would it cost?
多少錢？

例 How much is the fare?
票價多少？

例 What will the total fee be?
總共的費用是多少？

使用最頻繁的 旅遊英語

例	Is the admission included?
	門票都有包括在內嗎？
例	What's the price for an adult?
	成人票是多少錢？
例	Does it include lunch?
	有包含午餐嗎？

關鍵單字

sea cruise 海上遊艇行程

all-inclusive 一切計算在內的、包括一切的

round-trip fare 來回車資費用

pick up service 接送服務

基本句型

Where can I take a taxi?

我可以在哪裡招到計程車？

實用會話

A Do you need any help?
需要幫助嗎？

B Yes, I am lost. Do you know where the Museum is?
是的，我迷路了。你知道博物館在哪裡嗎？

A Oh, it's pretty far away from here.
喔，那裡離這裡很遠。

B Where can I take a taxi?
我可以在哪裡招到計程車？

A The taxi stand is right on the corner.
計程車招呼站就在街角。

B Thank you very much.
非常謝謝你。

相關例句

例 Where is the taxi stand?
計程車招呼站在哪裡？

關鍵單字

far away from 到某地是遙遠的
taxi stand 計程車招呼站(等計程車的地方)

 基本句型

Can you get me out of here?

你能不能載我去那邊？

 實用會話

A	Where to, sir? 先生，你要去哪裡？
B	Can you get me out of here? 你能不能載我去那邊？
A	Please get in. 請上車。
B	How far is it from here? 從這裡過去有多遠？
A	Well, It's about 5 miles. 嗯…大約有五哩。
B	Can you get me to there in twenty minutes? 你可以在二十分鐘內送我到達嗎？

 相關例句

例	Could you call me a cab? 可以幫我叫計程車嗎？
例	Please to this place. （拿出地圖或紙條）請到這個地方。
例	City Hall, please. 請（載我）到市政廳。

例　Please get me to the City Hall.
請載我到市政廳。

例　Can I get a cab around here?
這附近可以叫到計程車嗎？

關鍵單字

get me out　載我至某地
mile　哩

使用最頻繁的 旅遊英語

 基本句型

How long will it take?

需要多久的時間？

 實用會話

A Where to, madam?
女士，請問去哪裡？

B Please take me to the airport.
請送我到機場。

A OK.
好的。

B Excuse me, how long will it take?
請問一下，需要多久的時間？

A It's about 30 minutes.
大約卅分鐘。

B Please hurry. I have to catch a 10 o'clock plane.
請快一點！我要趕搭十點的飛機。

A Yes, madam.
是的，女士。

 相關例句

例 How long does it take to get there?
到那裡要多久的時間？

Unit 114 到達目的地

 基本句型

Drop us off at the next corner.

讓我們在下個轉角下車！

 實用會話

A Where to?
要去哪裡？

B Please take us to Maple Street.
請載我們到楓葉街！

A Yes, sir.
好的，先生。

B Drop us off at the next corner.
讓我們在下個轉角下車！

A Here we are. It's five hundred dollars.
到了！總共是五百元。

B Keep the change.
不用找零了！

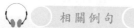 相關例句

例 Please let me off in front of it.
我讓我它的前面下車。

例 Stop at the next corner, please.
請在下個轉角停車！

 關鍵單字

off 下車

Unit 115 計程車資

基本句型

How much is the fare?

車資是多少？

實用會話

A How long does it take to get there?
到那裡要多久的時間？

B It's about 50 minutes.
大概五十分鐘。

A I see. Thank you.
我了解了。謝謝你。

（稍後到達目的地）

B Here you are.
到了。

A How much is the fare?
車資是多少？

B It's two hundred and fifty dollars.
總共二百五十元。

相關例句

例 What's the fare?
車資是多少？

例 How much?
多少錢？

例 How much does it cost to get to the airport?
到機場要多少錢？

搭車

🎧 基本句型

I am lost.

我迷路了。

🎧 實用會話

A Excuse me, I am lost.
抱歉，我迷路了。

B Where are you going?
你要去哪裡？

A Would you tell me how to go to the Railway Station?
你能告訴我如何去火車站嗎？

B Go straight ahead about four blocks and turn left. You will see it.
直走過四個街段再左轉，你就會看到(火車站)。

A What are the landmarks around the station?
車站附近有沒有明顯的建築物？

B There is a red building next to the station.
車站旁有一棟紅色的建築物。

🎧 相關例句

例 I don't know where I am.
我不知我人在哪裡。

例 Could you show me the direction?
可以指點我方向嗎？

使用最頻繁的 旅遊英語

 基本句型

How many stops are there to Seattle?

到西雅圖有多少個站？

 實用會話

A How many stops are there to Seattle?
到西雅圖有多少個站？

B That's the sixth stop.
那是第六站。

A Would you please tell me when we get there?
我們到達時可否告訴我一聲？

B Of course.
當然好。

(稍後到達目的地)

It's Seattle.
西雅圖到了。

A Let me off here, please.
我要在這裡下車。

 相關例句

例 Where does the bus for downtown leave from?
到市中心的巴士在哪裡發車？

例 How often does the bus for downtown leave?
到市中心的巴士多久來一班？

搭車

例　Where can I buy a ticket?
我可以在哪裡買到票？

例　Does this bus stop at the Museum?
巴士有停靠在博物館嗎？

例　Will you let me know when the bus arrives there?
可以告訴我巴士幾點會抵達那裡嗎？

 關鍵單字

stop　站別、停車站牌

使用最頻繁的 旅遊英語

 基本句型

I'm just looking.

我只是隨意看看。

 實用會話

A May I help you?
需要我幫忙的嗎？

B I'm just looking.
我只是隨意看看。

A Sure. Please let me know if you need anything.
好的！如果你需要任何東西的話，讓我知道一下。

B May I look at this one? I can't find it on the shelf.
我可以看一下這一個嗎？我在架上找不到這個。

A OK. Let me take a new one for you.
可以的。我拿一個新的給你。

 相關例句

例 I'm just browsing.
我只是參觀看看。

例 I just look around.
我只是看一看。

例 Can I take a look at this?
我可以看一看這個嗎？

買特定商品

 基本句型

I'm looking for a monitor.

我想買一個電腦螢幕。

 實用會話

A May I help you?
需要我幫忙的嗎？

B I'm looking for a monitor.
我想買一個電腦螢幕。

A Which brand do you want?
你想要什麼品牌？

B Panasonic. I want the same style as this one.
國際牌。我要和這個一樣的款式。

A Sorry, sir, it's out of stock.
抱歉，先生，這個沒有庫存了！

B Do you have a catalogue that I could see?
你們有目錄給我看看嗎？

A No problem. I'll be right back with you.
沒問題！我馬上回來。

 相關例句

例 Is this the best one you have?
這是你們有的最好的商品嗎？

例 This is what I want.
這就是我要的。

買特定商品

使用最頻繁的 旅遊英語

例 I'm looking for some suntan lotion.
我正在找一些防曬乳。

例 Do you have any one like this?
你們有賣像這一個的嗎?

例 I'd like to see some Mac lipsticks.
我想看一些Mac的口紅。

關鍵單字

out of stock 沒有庫存

catalogue 目錄

Unit 120 商品的售價

 基本句型

How much is it?

要多少錢？

 實用會話

A Please show me that black sweater.
請給我看看那件黑色毛衣。

B Here you are.
請看。

A How much is it?
要多少錢？

B It's two thousand dollars.
要兩千元。

A It's too expensive.
它太貴了。

 相關例句

例 How much did you say?
你說要多少錢？

例 What is the price?
價格是多少？

例 How much does it sell for?
它要賣多少錢？

使用最頻繁的 旅遊英語

例 How much is it together?
總共要多少錢？

例 How much does it cost?
這個賣多少錢？

例 How much shall I pay for it?
我應該要付多少錢？

基本句型

Is this item on sale this week?

這項商品本週有特價嗎？

 實用會話

A Does the closeout start today?
跳樓大拍賣是今天開始嗎？

B Yes, sir.
是的，先生。

A Is this item on sale this week?
這項商品本週有特價嗎？

B Yes, it's only five hundred dollars.
有的，只要五百元。

A When does this promotion end?
這個促銷什麼時候結束？

B Next Friday.
下週五。

 相關例句

例 Is this one on sale?
這個有特價嗎？

例 Is this hair dryer on clearance sale?
這個頭髮吹風機有在清倉特賣嗎？

例 Are they half off?
他們都賣半價嗎？

使用最頻繁的 旅遊英語

例　Can I use the coupon for that?
　　我可以用折價券買這個嗎？

例　May I have a rain check for this?
　　我可以改天用同樣價格買這個商品嗎？

不滿意商品

 基本句型

I like the style, but not the color.

我喜歡這款式，但是不喜歡這顏色。

 實用會話

A What do you think?
你覺得呢？

B The color is too light for the winter.
冬天穿這件衣服顏色太淺了。

A Yeah, I like the style, but not the color.
是啊！我喜歡這款式，但是不喜歡這顏色。

B How about this red one?
這個紅色的怎麼樣？

A This is what I want. It looks very nice.
這就是我要的。看起來很漂亮。

B Wonderful. It looks great on you.
太好了！你穿起來很好看。

 相關例句

例 I don't like the color.
我不喜歡這個顏色。

例 Any other colors?
有沒有其他顏色？

例 Do you have any other colors?
有沒有其他別的顏色？

不滿意商品

例　I don't think this is good.
　　我不覺得這件好。

例　It's a bit showy.
　　有點華麗。

Unit 123 試穿衣物

 基本句型

Can I try that on?

我可以試穿那件嗎？

 實用會話

A Can I try that on?
我可以試穿那件嗎？

B Sure. This way, please.
當然可以。這邊請。

A How does this look on me?
我穿這件看起來怎麼樣？

B Don't you think the waistline is too loose?
你不會覺得腰圍太鬆了嗎？

A Can I try a smaller one?
我能試穿較小件的嗎？

B Size 6, I guess.
我猜你要穿六號！

 相關例句

例 It's too tight.
太緊了。

例 It's still too tight around the stomach.
腰部太緊了。

例 It's too tight around the hip.
臀部太緊了。

使用最頻繁的 旅遊英語

例 It's too short.
太短了。

例 Do you have size 8?
你們有八號嗎？

例 Do you have free tailoring?
你們有免費修改嗎？

例 Could you adjust the length of the pants?
你能修改褲子的長度嗎？

Unit 124 詢問商品的尺寸

  逛街

 基本句型

Do you have this skirt in size seven?

這件裙子有七號尺寸嗎？

實用會話

A It looks perfect to me.
這個看起來很棒！

B Would you like to try it on?
你要試穿嗎？

A Do you have this skirt in size seven?
這件裙子有七號尺寸嗎？

B This comes in several sizes.
這有好多種尺寸。

A Let me see the red one, in my size, please.
請拿件紅色的給我看看，要合我的尺寸。

B Sure.
好的。

相關例句

例 I want the large size.
我要大尺寸的。

例 I don't know what my size is.
我不知道我的尺寸。

例 This is not my size.
這不是我的尺寸。

是否有折扣

使用最頻繁的 旅遊 英語

 基本句型

Any discount?

有沒有折扣？

 實用會話

A How much is it?
這個賣多少錢？

B It's five thousand dollars.
五千元。

A I'd like something cheaper. Any discount?
我想買一些較便宜的。有沒有折扣？

B I'm afraid not, madam.
抱歉，女士，沒有。

A I can't afford that! It cost me an arm and a leg.
我付不起！真是貴得要命。

 相關例句

例 Can you cut me a deal?
你可以算我便宜一點嗎？

例 Can you give me a discount?
你可以給我折扣嗎？

例 Can you come down a little?
可以再便宜一點嗎？

附錄　關鍵單字總匯

【證件】

passport	護照
passport number	護照號碼
visa	簽證
visa number	簽證號碼
student visa	學生簽證
business visa	商務簽證
sightseeing visa	觀光簽證
valid	有效
invalid	逾期無效
issue place	發照地
day of issue	發照日期
travel document	旅行文件

【機票】

airfare	票價
ticket	機票
one-way ticket	單程票
round-trip ticket	來回票
non-stop	直達
stop-over	轉機
round-trip	來回旅程
one-way trip	單程旅程
arrival	入境
departure	出境
on time	準時
take off	起飛
landing	著陸
confirm	確認

【班次】

airlines	航空公司
flight	航班
non-stop flight	直達航班
stop-over flight	轉機航班
domestic flight	國內線
international flight	國際線
regular flight	定期班次
extra flight	臨時班次

【航班】

timetable	時刻表
local time	當地時間
departure time	離境時間
arrive	抵達
delay	延誤

【在機場】

check in	報到
airport	機場
arrival lobby	入境大廳
check-in counter	報到櫃檯
entrance	入口
exit	出口
smoking room	吸煙室
information desk	服務台
ATM	自動提款機
post office	郵局
public telephone	公共電話

bank	銀行	business class	商務艙
duty-free shop	免稅商店	economy class	經濟艙
restaurant	餐廳		

		【轉機】	
coffee shop	咖啡廳	transfer	轉機
elevator	電梯	transit	過境
escalator	手扶梯	shuttle bus	接駁車
stairs	樓梯	VIP lounges	貴賓室
restroom	廁所	waiting room	候機室
ladies' room	女廁	greeting area	到站等候區

gentlemen's room	男廁		
public phone	公用電話	【兌換貨幣】	
long distance call	長途電話	pay	支付
international call	國際電話	tax	稅務
busy line	佔線中	cash	現金
parking lot	停車場	coin	硬幣

【行李】		exchange	兌換
baggage / luggage	行李	exchange rate	兌換稅率
carry-on bag	手提行李	small change	零錢
baggage delivcry	行李托運	bill	紙鈔
baggage claim	提領行李區	airport tax	機場稅
claim tag	托運行李卡	commission	手續費

coin locker	寄物櫃	【人物】	
luggage scale	行李磅秤	passenger	乘客
luggage tag	行李標籤	traveler	旅客
luggage trolley	行李手推車	captain	機長

【登機】		flight attendant	空服員
board	登機	airline staff	地勤人員
boarding gate	登機門	companion	同伴
Gate 4	4號登機門	acquaintance	認識者
boarding pass	登機證		
first class	頭等艙		

【在飛機上】

seat	座位
aisle seat	走道座位
window seat	靠窗座位
smoking area	吸煙區
non-smoking area	非吸煙區
emergency exit	緊急出口
head sets	耳機
airsick	暈機的
headache	頭痛
pain	疼痛
stomachache	胃痛
fever	發燒
thirsty	口渴的
blanket	毯子
pillow	枕頭
aspirin	阿司匹靈
meal	餐點
drink	飲料
movie	電影
occupied	(廁所)使用中
vacant	(廁所)無人使用
overhead cabinet	上方櫃子
fasten	繫緊
seatbelt	安全帶
life vest	救生衣
oxygen mask	氧氣面罩
fasten seat belt	扣緊安全帶
airsickness bags	嘔吐袋
turbulence	亂流
temperature	氣溫
local time	當地時間
jet lag	時差

【在海關】

immigration officer	移民官
customs officer	海關官員
quarantine officer	檢疫官
visa-exempted try	免簽入境
expired overstay	逾期滯留
overstay	逾期
destination	目的地
pass through	過境
prohibited items	違禁品
declare	申報
fill in	填寫
immigration	入境檢查
passport control	護照檢查
embarkation card	入境記錄卡
customs declaration card	
	海關申報單
currency declaration	現金申報單
application form	申請表
full name	全名
identification card	身份證
occupation	職業
address	住址
nationality	國籍
register	登記
prohibited articles	違禁品
duty-free items	免稅品
quarantine	檢疫
residents	本國居民
Non-residents	外國居民
transit passenger	過境旅客
interpreter	翻譯人員
stamp	章戳

【訂房】

check in	登記住宿
check out	退房
vacancy	空房
available	空房的
confirmation slip	確認單
counter	櫃臺
operator	總機
receptionist	接待員
single room	單人房
double room	雙人房
sauna	蒸氣
view	景觀
reservation	預約
cancel	取消
check	確認
book	預訂

【在飯店】

key	鑰匙
room number	房號
floor	樓層
lobby	大廳
laundry service	洗衣服務
laundry	送洗的衣服
cleaners	乾洗店
locker	衣物櫃
message	信息
souvenir	紀念品
tourist attractions	觀光名勝
room service	房間服務
wake-up call	早晨叫醒服務
tip	小費

【費用】

room rate	房價
charge	收費
cost	花費
bill	帳單
credit card	信用卡
cash	現金
traveler's check	旅行支票
receipt	收據
coupon	配給券

【旅遊】

map	地圖
travel tour	旅行團
sightseeing tour	觀光旅遊團
souvenir	紀念品
guide books	指南手冊
tour brochure	旅遊手冊
scenic spots	觀光景點
tour guide	導遊

商業實用英文 E-mail 業務篇(50 開)

最權威、最具說服力的商用英文 E-mail 書信，馬上搶救職場上的英文書信寫作。史上最強的商用英文 E-mail！三大特色：1000 句商用英文 E-mail+例句 500 個商用英文 E-mail 關鍵單字+33 篇商用英文 E-mail 範例。最搶手的商用英文寶典，提升實力就從「商業實用英文 E-mail（業務篇）」開始。

求職面試必備英文 附 MP3(50 開)

六大步驟，讓你英文求職高人一等馬上搶救職場的英文面試全國第一本針對「應徵面試」的英文全集！三大特色：三大保證：三大機會：成功升遷成功覓得新工作成功開創海外事業新契機學習英文最快的工具書，利用「情境式對話」，讓您英文會話能力突飛猛進！

Goodmorning 很生活的英語(50 開)

"超實用超廣泛超好記好背、好學、生活化，最能讓你朗朗上口的英語。日常生活中，人們要透過互相問候來保持一種良好的社會關係。因此，只要一聲 Good morning, Hello, Hi!不但拉近你和朋友的距離，更能為自己的人際關係加分。英語不能死背，用生活化的方式學英語，才能克服開不了口的窘境！"

遊學必備 1500 句(50 開)

留學˙移民˙旅行美國生活最常用的生活會話！遊學學生必備生活寶典，完全提升遊學過程中的語言能力，讓您順利完成遊學夢想！

超簡單的旅遊英語 (附 MP3)(50 開)

出國再也不必比手劃腳，出國再也不怕鴨子聽雷簡單一句話，勝過背卻派不上用場的單字，適用於所有在國外旅遊的對話情境。

出國前記得一定要帶的東西：*護照*旅費*個人物品*超簡單的旅遊英語適用範圍*出國旅遊*自助旅行*出國出差*短期遊學…

商業祕書英文 E-mail (50 開)

商業祕書英文 E-mail**英文寫作速成班**?我也可以是英文書寫高手！明天就要寫一封信外國客戶了，卻不知道該如何下筆嗎？？本書提供完整的 E-mail 書信範例，讓您輕輕鬆鬆完成 E-mail 書信

菜英文-基礎實用篇 (50 開)

沒有英文基礎發音就不能說英文嗎？不必怕！只要你會中文，一樣可以順口ㄅㄠˊ英文！學英文一點都不難！生活常用語句輕鬆說！只要你開口跟著念，說英文不再是難事！

如何上英文網站購物 (50 開)

上外國網站血拼、訂房、買機票…英文網站購物一指通！利用最短的時間，快速上網搜尋資料、提出問題、下單、結帳…從此之後，不必擔心害怕上外國網站購物！

出差英文 1000 句型
(附 MP3)(50 開)

出差英語例句寶典完整度百分百！實用度百分百！簡單一句話，勝過千言萬語的說明！適用於所有國外出差的情境。

脫口說英語(基礎篇)
(附 MP3)-50K

1500 句超實用短句臨時需要說英語，也能輕鬆脫口說英語！10 種問候的短句 How are you? How are you doing? How are you going today? How do you do? How have you been? How is it going? How is everything? Is everything OK? How are things going? How is it going?

1000 基礎實用單字
(附 MP3)-50K

只要掌握基礎單字，輕鬆開口說英語！蒐集使用最頻繁的 1000 單字，編撰最實用、最好記、最能朗朗上口的口語英文

商業實用英文 E-mail-
業務篇(48K)

E-mail 商用書信 No.1 的選擇！分門別類規劃商務主題，查詢方便主題、例句馬上套用，快速完成一封商務 E-mail 信件

出差英文一把罩(48K)

出差、商務、談判商務會話 NO.1 的選擇！不必靠翻譯，三言兩語就能搞定外籍客戶，用簡單的英文實力，快速提升職場競爭力！

菜英文
【旅遊實用篇】-50K

就算是說得一口的菜英文，也能出國自助旅行！本書提供超強的中文發音輔助，教您輕輕鬆鬆暢遊全球！

生活英語萬用手冊
(附 MP3)(48K)

英語學習不再是紙上談兵！背誦單字的同時，也能學習生活中最常用的短語對話，讓英語學習更佳生活化、更有效率！

我的菜英文
【單字篇】

英文開口說 音譯寶典全方位英文口語學習，不用高學歷也會開口說英語！不必再從頭學音標了利用中文發音學習英文快速克服發音的障礙。

英語這樣說最正確
(MP3)-50K

徹底擺脫英語學習的障礙！利用動詞片語串連式的學習法，快速掌握英語單字、生動的動詞片語應用，有助於增進開口說英語的技巧！沒有艱深的單字，但是你知道以下的英文是什麼意思嗎？Have a nice day. Take it or leave it.Now you're talking! Don't be such a poor loser.I don't have a clue.

國家圖書館出版品預行編目資料

使用最頻繁的旅遊英語／張瑜凌編著.
--初版. --臺北縣汐止市：雅典文化,民98.01
面；公分. --（實用會話系列：8）
ISBN：978-986-7041-72-2 (平裝附光碟片)
1. 英語　　2. 旅遊　　3. 會話
805.188　　　　　　　　　　　97023130

實用會話系列：8

使用最頻繁的旅遊英語

編　　著◎張瑜凌

出 版 者◎雅典文化事業有限公司

登 記 證◎局版北市業字第五七〇號

發 行 人◎黃玉雲

執行編輯◎張瑜凌

編 輯 部◎221 台北縣汐止市大同路三段 194-1 號 9 樓

電　　話◎02-86473663　傳真◎02-86473660

郵　　撥◎18965580 雅典文化事業有限公司

法律顧問◎永信法律事務所　林永頌律師

總 經 銷◎永續圖書有限公司

　　　　　221 台北縣汐止市大同路三段 194-1 號 9 樓

　　　　　EmailAdd: yungjiuh@ms45.hinet.net

　　　　　網站◎ www.foreverbooks.com.tw

　　　　　郵撥◎ 18669219

　　　　　電話◎ 02-86473663　傳真◎ 02-86473660

初　　版◎2009 年 01 月

定　　價◎ NT$ 250 元

雅典文化 **讀者回函卡**

> 謝謝您購買這本書。
> 為加強對讀者的服務，請您詳細填寫本卡，寄回**雅典文化**；並請務必留下您的E-mail帳號，我們會主動將最近"好康"的促銷活動告訴您，保證值回票價。

書　　名：使用最頻繁的旅遊英語

購買書店：＿＿＿＿＿市／縣＿＿＿＿＿＿＿＿書店

姓　　名：＿＿＿＿＿＿＿＿　生　日：＿＿年＿月＿日

身分證字號：＿＿＿＿＿＿＿＿＿＿＿＿＿

電　　話：(私)＿＿＿＿(公)＿＿＿＿(手機)＿＿＿＿

地　　址：□□□＿＿＿＿＿＿＿＿＿＿＿＿

E - mail：＿＿＿＿＿＿＿＿＿＿＿＿＿＿

年　　齡：□20歲以下　□21歲～30歲　□31歲～40歲
　　　　　□41歲～50歲　□51歲以上

性　　別：□男　□女　　婚姻：□單身　□已婚

職　　業：□學生　　□大眾傳播　□自由業　□資訊業
　　　　　□金融業　□銷售業　　□服務業　□教職
　　　　　□軍警　　□製造業　　□公職　　□其他

教育程度：□高中以下（含高中）□大專　□研究所以上

職 位 別：□負責人　□高階主管　□中級主管
　　　　　□一般職員□專業人員

職 務 別：□管理　　□行銷　　□創意　　□人事、行政
　　　　　□財務、法務　　□生產　　□工程　　□其他＿＿＿＿＿＿

您從何得知本書消息？
　　　　□逛書店　　□報紙廣告　□親友介紹
　　　　□出版書訊　□廣告信函　□廣播節目
　　　　□電視節目　□銷售人員推薦
　　　　□其他＿＿＿＿＿＿＿＿

您通常以何種方式購書？
　　　　□逛書店　　□劃撥郵購　□電話訂購　□傳真訂購　□信用卡
　　　　□團體訂購　□網路書店　□其他＿＿＿＿＿＿＿＿

看完本書後，您喜歡本書的理由？
　　　　□內容符合期待　□文筆流暢　□具實用性　□插圖生動
　　　　□版面、字體安排適當　　□內容充實
　　　　□其他＿＿＿＿＿＿＿＿

看完本書後，您不喜歡本書的理由？
　　　　□內容不符合期待　□文筆欠佳　　□內容平平
　　　　□版面、圖片、字體不適合閱讀　　□觀念保守
　　　　□其他＿＿＿＿＿＿＿＿

您的建議：＿＿＿＿＿＿＿＿＿＿＿＿
＿＿＿＿＿＿＿＿＿＿＿＿＿＿＿＿

廣 告 回 信

基隆郵局登記證

基隆廣字第 056 號

2 2 1 - 0 3

台北縣汐止市大同路三段 194 號 9 樓之 1

雅典文化事業有限公司

編輯部　收

請沿此虛線對折免貼郵票，以膠帶黏貼後寄回，謝謝！

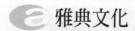

雅典文化

為你開啟知識之殿堂